ANY

WHICH

WALL

ALSO BY LAUREL SNYDER

ANY WHICH WALL

LAUREL SNYDER

RANDOM HOUSE
NEW YORK

DRAWINGS BY
LEUYEN PHAM

This is a work of fiction. Names, characters, places, and incidents either are the product of the author's imagination or are used fictitiously. Any resemblance to actual persons, living or dead, events, or locales is entirely coincidental.

Text copyright © 2009 by Laurel Snyder
Illustrations copyright © 2009 by LeUyen Pham

Published in the United States by Random House Children's Books,
a division of Random House, Inc., New York.

Random House and colophon are registered trademarks of Random House, Inc.

Visit us on the Web! www.randomhouse.com/kids

Educators and librarians, for a variety of teaching tools,
visit us at www.randomhouse.com/teachers

Visit www.laurelsnyder.com

Library of Congress Cataloging-in-Publication Data
Snyder, Laurel.
Any which wall / Laurel Snyder. — 1st ed.
p. cm.
Summary: In the middle of an Iowa cornfield, four children find a magic wall
that enables them to travel through time and space.
ISBN 978-0-375-85560-3 (trade) — ISBN 978-0-375-95560-0 (lib. bdg.) —
ISBN 978-0-375-85383-8 (e-book)
[1. Magic—Fiction. 2. Wishes—Fiction. 3. Space and time—Fiction.
4. Brothers and sisters—Fiction. 5. Iowa—Fiction.] I. Title.
PZ7.S6851764An 2009
[Fic]—dc22
2008022605

Printed in the United States of America
10 9 8 7 6 5 4 3 2 1
First Edition

To Henry and Emma and Susan and Roy.
And to Chris, Mose, and Lew.
I love you guys.

Contents

"The best kind of magic book," Barnaby was saying,
"is the kind where the magic has rules.
And you have to deal with it and thwart it
before it thwarts you. Only sometimes
you forget and get thwarted."

—*Seven Day Magic*, Edward Eager

A BRIEF NOTE ON THE EXISTENCE
AND TRUE NATURE OF MAGIC

Have you ever stumbled onto magic? Maybe while you were trudging to school one drizzly day, or in the middle of a furious game of freeze tag? Has anything odd ever happened to you?

If you're shaking your head right now, if you think that nothing out of the ordinary ever happens, you might be mistaken. Because it's possible that you stumbled onto magic and missed it—that you were teetering on the edge of a strange and wonderful adventure but then turned the other way. This happens all the time.

I know a boy (we'll call him Horbert, though that isn't his name, thank goodness), and for years he lived in a house where the bathtub had a magical drainpipe that led straight to the lost city of Atlantis! But Horbert was always in such a hurry to get where he was going that he never lingered in the bath. Whenever he got really filthy, and his mother nagged him to wash, he just jumped in and briefly splashed at himself.

Then he'd spring right from the tub, and out the door he'd fly, afraid that his older brother Noah was beating his high score on Super-Space-Zombie-4000, his very favorite video game. Though mermaids sang in the plumbing, he never heard their call.

This is sad but not uncommon, so maybe you need to ask yourself whether you're in danger of becoming a little like Horbert. These days, most people are. Most people are just too busy for magic—watching TV and checking their e-mail—so it stands to reason that when something unusual happens, folks are often looking the other way.

You might think that magic would be too extraordinary to miss. You might be saying, "Oh, trust me, if I stumbled onto magic, I'd know it!" But that's not necessarily true. Because there are many kinds of magic in the world, and not all of it starts with a sound track of thunderous music to alert unsuspecting explorers to fabulous adventures ahead.

Some magic (the kind you hear about most often) is loud and full of dragons. But that magic is rare, generally reserved for scrappy orphans and misplaced princes. Some magic is mysterious, beginning with the somber tolling of a clock at midnight in the darkest corner of a graveyard. However, that magic is unlikely to include you if you don't visit cemeteries late at night (which I don't think you're supposed to do). There is also magic especially for very tiny children, full of kindly rabbits and friendly old ladies with comfortable laps. It smells like sugar cookies and takes place mostly in gardens or bedrooms the pale colors of spring. But you outgrow it about the time you learn to read.

So perhaps the very best magic is the kind of magic that happens to kids just like you (and maybe even the occasional grown-up) when they're paying careful attention. It's the most common magic there is, which is why (sensibly) it's called *Common Magic. Common Magic* exists in the very unmagical world you yourself inhabit. It's full of regular-looking people, stop signs, and seemingly boring buildings. *Common Magic* happens to kids who have curious friends, busy parents, and vivid imaginations, and it frequently takes place during summer vacations or on rainy weekends when you aren't allowed to leave the house. Most important, it always starts with something that seems ordinary.

This magic, the magic in this particular book, was *Common Magic.* It happened last July, to Henry and Emma, and Susan and Roy, and it started with a wall. . . .

In Quiet Falls

BUT FIRST everybody had to *find* the wall . . . and that might never have even happened if Emma O'Dell hadn't learned to ride her bike. So if you think about it, the magic *really* started with a bicycle.

It was summer in Iowa, and for the first two weeks of vacation, Emma and her older brother, Henry, just hung around the house because their parents were too busy with work, and silly things like mowing the lawn, to take Henry and Emma to the beach or the mountains, or even to the park for a picnic. Henry and Emma were free from school but stuck at home.

Often the two of them played halfhearted games of Parcheesi, and that was fine but nothing special. Sometimes they started a game of Don't Touch the Floor, but it wasn't much fun without their mom around to yell at them for thumping and knocking things over.

Then, at the beginning of the third week, Emma learned to ride the shiny green bike she'd gotten for her sixth birthday only the month before, and that's when the summer opened up like a giant map unfolding—full of mud puddles and climbing trees and trips to the library. That's when vacation really began, since Henry and Emma were allowed to ride anywhere they wanted in Quiet Falls, as long as Henry kept a careful eye on his sister and called to check in occasionally. Quiet Falls was a friendly town, and the O'Dells knew everyone in it, so nobody worried too much.

"Why don't Mom and Dad ever ride *their* bikes?" Emma asked Henry one early afternoon of bicycle freedom, over gooey pizza at Pagliano's. "Maybe they'd like to come with us sometime?" As a rule, Emma asked a lot of questions. There was something in her upturned nose and big blue eyes that made her look as though she were *always* about to ask a question.

Henry shook his head. "Nah. Parents are kind of lazy when it comes to doing fun stuff outdoors."

"Then why do they have bikes?" asked Emma.

"That's just how parents are," Henry explained wisely as he ate the cheese off the top of his slice and wiped his greasy hand on his jeans. "They like to talk about how they *used* to do things or about how they plan to do things *someday,* but parents aren't very good at *right now.*"

Henry thought about this for a bit and sighed in a mildly disappointed way. He often wished his parents were more exciting. Both of them were pharmacists, and he couldn't think of anything more boring than that. It would be so cool to be the son of a mad scientist and a famous explorer!

"Oh." Emma nodded and went back to sprinkling too much garlic salt on her pizza. It was nice to sit like this, alone with Henry. Often Henry's friend Roy was with them, and though the boys were nice enough to Emma, they sometimes forgot to include her.

Roy Levy was Henry's best friend and next-door neighbor since forever. They'd been born in the same hospital, just fourteen days apart. They'd been in the same fourth-grade class last year, and they were on the same soccer team. Roy and Henry even looked a little alike. They were the same height, with the same mousy shade of brown hair, and the same brown eyes. However, that was where the resemblance stopped, because while Henry was "trouble, and a mess to boot" (his grandma said so), Roy was the kind of boy that grown-ups like— quiet and curious. But don't get the wrong idea about Roy—even though he kept his shirts clean, Roy was a lot of fun, so Henry and Emma were generally happy to have him on their jaunts, and they all enjoyed themselves in a summery kind of way.

This might have continued indefinitely if at the end of the fourth week of vacation Roy hadn't gotten stung seven times by what he called *Apis mellifera* (though they looked a lot like plain old bees to Henry and Emma) during a raspberry raid in a thicket at the park. This caused Mrs. Levy to have a talk with Mr. O'Dell, which resulted in a decision—that Roy's older sister, Susan, should follow along to keep an eye on everyone *at all times.*

Susan was only two years older than Roy, and until the previous summer, she and her best friend, Tish, had been happy to join in most of Henry and Roy and

Emma's games. The big girls had liked being in charge—dressing Emma in costumes, bossing the boys around in games of make-believe—but then Tish had moved to New York, and Susan had . . . changed. The problem wasn't that she'd gotten taller so that her legs suddenly appeared too long. It wasn't that she'd cut her long, dark braids into a bob that ended at a sharp point near her chin. It wasn't even that she'd started wearing nail polish and carrying a pink cell phone. It was simply that she didn't play with Roy and Henry and Emma anymore, that she didn't *play* at all, preferring instead to "hang out" with other middle schoolers.

At first, when her mother announced that she'd be spending the summer watching Henry, Emma, and Roy, Susan complained loudly and bitterly, but when she realized that her new best friend, Alexandria, was going to be spending July and August with her father in Chicago, Susan became instantly less miserable at the prospect of babysitting. She didn't have much else to do, so she dug her bike out from under a pile of garden hose in the garage and dusted it off.

Then, together, the four of them rode aimlessly to the lake and to the store for provisions (candy and soda). They rode to the library and to the swimming pool, and it was fun, but just regular old fun, *common* fun. Henry hopped a lot of curbs and fell down more than a few times, and Roy found a praying mantis, which he kept in a jar.

And if lakes and libraries don't sound exciting to you, if they don't sound magical to you, you need to remember that this adventure is one of Common Magic. Henry and Emma and Roy and Susan had yet to *find* the wall, but they *were* on their way, heading slowly toward it.

The wall was waiting for them, just like it's waiting for you now.

Still, it must be admitted that none of the kids had any inkling of what lay ahead, until Tuesday, when it was too hot to do anything. It was too hot for board games and it was even too hot to ride to the pool, so they were all doing nothing at Henry and Emma's house. They did nothing in the living room, and they did nothing in the kitchen, where they ate a nothing kind of lunch—tuna fish sandwiches and carrot sticks. Blah.

After that, they sat on the front porch doing a little more nothing. Susan wiped imaginary specks of dust from her silver sneakers and tried tying her laces in a cool new way. Roy made a sundial out of a sheet of paper and a paper clip. And Henry perched at the bottom of the steps, where he attempted to pull a wad of gum out of his sweaty, messy brown hair.

"That's revolting," Susan offered helpfully, looking up from her shoes.

"Well, what do you want me to do about it? I'm *trying* to get it out," said Henry.

"You should just cut it out," said Susan, "so we don't have to watch you play with it anymore."

"I'm not *playing* with it, and I'm *not* cutting my hair. I did that last time, and it looked stupid. Remember?" Henry stopped fiddling for a minute and the shock of hair in question stood straight up in the air so that thin strands of gum were laced across his entire head.

Susan laughed.

"What?" asked Henry indignantly. "What's so funny?"

"Just you," Susan snickered.

"Leave me alone," Henry grumbled. "I guess I'm just not magically clean like you."

"It's not magic," said Susan, shaking her hair from side to side slowly so that it swished around her chin, "and I don't pretend to be perfect. It's just that I'm"— she thought for a second before continuing—"more mature."

Henry groaned. "Jeez. You don't have to tell *me* you aren't perfect, and I know it isn't magic either, since there's no such thing as magic, but what do you want to go and get *mature* for?"

Susan, despite her newfound maturity, stuck out her tongue before she said, "I *have* to act like this, you know. I'm in charge. Of *you*! Remember?"

Henry groaned. "I know you have to babysit us, but there's a big difference between being in charge for a few hours and acting like a grown-up. Don't you remember all the cool stuff you used to do? You used to be fun."

Henry paused, waiting for Susan to snap back, but she just looked down the street in the direction of Tish's old house.

Henry quit tugging at his hair and sighed.

Roy, who had been listening and thinking, looked up from his sundial and said, "You know, I'm not so sure—"

"About what?" asked Henry.

"About magic, that there's no such thing," said Roy.

"Are you *kidding*?!" Henry exclaimed with a hoot. "Just because Susan's acting all old doesn't mean *you* have to suddenly turn into a baby! Come on, you don't actually believe in *magic*?"

"Well," said Roy, "I don't know if I *believe* in magic, but I'm not ready to rule it out completely."

Susan looked up. "Really, Roy? Have you ever seen any magic?"

"No," said Roy simply. "But wouldn't it be nice if magic *did* exist?"

"Sure," said Henry. "But that's not proof. How can you believe in something you've never seen?"

Roy answered logically. "I've never seen atoms and electrons either, but I *believe* in them."

Henry thought about this. "So, you're really saying you think there might be dragons and unicorns running around?"

Susan waited to see what her brother would say.

"No, not dragons or unicorns," Roy explained thoughtfully. "They seem highly unlikely, since people would have hunted them down and put them in zoos centuries ago."

"Then what do you mean?" asked Susan, thinking of her old unicorn figurine collection and wondering vaguely if her mother had ever actually taken it to the Salvation Army, or if the little statues were somewhere in the basement. "What other kind of magic is there?" she asked her brother. "If there *is* magic, I mean—which there isn't."

"I don't know what I think exactly," Roy answered. "I haven't given it much thought. I'm just saying there's a lot of stuff out there that I don't understand, and people have been believing in magic for thousands of years, so it just seems . . . not *impossible*." He returned to his sundial, having finished making his point.

While all this was going on, Emma had been playing in the front yard with an oversized rag doll named Green Bean Jean. Green Bean Jean was almost as big as Emma and the color of a lime lollipop, with wild orange yarn hair.

Emma clutched Green Bean Jean's cloth hands in her own, and swayed back and forth, singing softly to herself. Nobody could make out the words, but halfway through the song, Emma dropped to the ground and brought Green Bean Jean down with her in a tumble onto the grass. Then she got up and began again.

Susan watched Emma's solitary game for a moment. Then she stood up, and it almost looked like she was going to walk down the steps and offer to play too. Emma, accustomed to playing alone, looked up hopefully, but Susan stared off into the distance absently, and the moment passed, so Emma dropped Green Bean Jean, climbed on her bike, and began to coast up and down the front walk.

After a minute, she called out, "Let's go somewhere!"

"Let's not," replied Henry grumpily, reconciling

himself to the idea that he would indeed have to cut the gum out of his hair. He sighed. "Hey, Susan, I give up. You want to cut my hair for me?"

Susan nodded, and though she still looked distracted, she walked over and picked up the scissors from where Roy had been working on his sundial. Susan liked to fix things.

"But I want to ride my bike!" protested Emma.

"So? You're doing that right now," said Henry.

"Nooooo. I want to ride it *to* someplace," explained Emma. "Pleeeeeeeease? You know I'm not allowed to leave the street on my own."

"No way. It's too hot," said her brother. "Wait until it cools off."

"Yeah, it's supposed to be ninety-nine degrees today," seconded Roy, "in the shade."

But Susan looked over at Emma, astride the small bike, and then at Green Bean Jean sprawled forlornly on the lawn. She smiled, then set down the scissors and said, "Oh, come on, everyone."

"Huh?" Henry said.

"Really?" Emma asked.

"It won't be too bad," Susan said. "At least it'll be breezy."

Fifteen minutes later, they all agreed that it *did* feel

breezy riding along the blacktop with the wind in their faces. They pedaled hard and then coasted with their legs stuck straight out (except Emma, who couldn't yet).

They rode east, past shops their mothers described as "adorable," stores that sold things like hand-knitted sweaters for cats. They passed a small park and then a bigger park. Beyond the two parks, they passed houses that got farther and farther apart and smaller and smaller, until finally there were no buildings left to look at, just green grass and gently rustling cornfields, and sky for miles.

Only a few minutes into the wonderful green of the fields, the asphalt beneath their bike tires turned to gravel. It made it hard to pedal, but that was fun in its own way too. The kids bumped along with gravel flying and clouds of dust puffing up at their knees. Emma sang a song, and even though it was a little-kid song about a farmer who had a dog (you probably know it), the others joined in.

Here, in the big open fields, as they pedaled and sang at the top of their lungs, the heat was somehow okay. It fit. The kids were sweating and red-faced, but it felt far better to be hot from doing *something* than hot from doing *nothing*.

When the gravel road ended at a tiny path, everyone

stopped pedaling and peered down the narrow dirt path. It was more than a little overgrown, with weeds snarled everywhere and the short cornstalks bent down into the path.

"Knee-high by the Fourth of July," chortled Emma.

"Except that it isn't," pointed out Henry. The corn came almost to Emma's waist. "Whatever old farmer invented that saying was a lot taller than you."

"Probably lots of poison ivy in there," Roy cautioned, leaning down to inspect.

"Yeah, so what now?" asked Henry, looking at Susan.

She was in charge, and they all knew she'd be in the deepest trouble if they weren't back before dinner, but really, there were only two choices: they could turn back, which none of them wanted to do, or they could follow the path that beckoned to them through the corn.

If you were Susan, what would you have done?

Well, I should hope so!

Flashing an excited grin, Susan tore off down the path on her bike, and with a loud whooping, the others followed. The cornstalks brushed against their legs as bugs cricketed and buzzed in the fields. They couldn't see any houses. They couldn't hear the road. There wasn't a single person in sight, not even a power line or a streetlight to disturb the enormous sky. The field felt amazing: all green waving fronds, with the big blue above. The kids lost themselves in it, bumping and yelling, pedaling as hard as they could.

Until they saw something. Something dark and tall looming ahead. Something that did not fit.

Susan stopped her bike and held up a hand to shade her eyes. She peered at the dark thing in the distance. "Is it a house?" she wondered aloud.

"I don't think so," answered Roy, bumping into her back tire as he coasted to a stop behind her. "It's too tall and thin for a house. Maybe it's just a shadow."

"Hey, guys, *guys*! What're you talking about? I can't see *anything*!" called Emma from the rear. She was too short to see over the heads of the other three. "Move, *please*!"

When the other three ducked down, Emma stared too.

Now, maybe you're confused by this part of the story. Maybe you think that if you saw a very big wall, dark in the distance, you'd simply say, "Look, everyone, a very big wall!" But Henry, Emma, Susan, and Roy had grown up in Quiet Falls, and even though they'd never ridden their bikes quite this far, they *had* wandered through a fair number of cornfields before. In all those years, they'd never seen a big stone wall in the middle of nowhere.

"We've come this far. No reason not to check it out," said Susan, placing her right foot firmly on its pedal.

This was the right thing for her to say. It was the thing she might not have said if she were a little more like Horbert, if she'd been rushing home to check her e-mail. Susan's words took them all into the adventure, and not home to their safe houses.

They pedaled forward slowly, and in a few minutes, the tall dark thing became a bigger dark thing. Finally it turned into a wall made of gray and black stones, heavy rough squares, each about the size of a large suit-case. As tall as City Hall and about that wide, the wall looked precarious, tilting toward them.

They all got off their bikes.

If the Key Fits

"Wow," said Henry, staring up.

Everyone agreed: the wall *was* "wow." It looked like something from another place and time, ancient and mysterious, leaning over them. They just stood. Gaping. Up.

"It's so big," said Roy after a while. "What do you think it *was*? I mean, what did it start out as, back when it was built?"

"A castle!" Emma answered right away with absolute certainty. "A big giant castle. For when people needed to hide from Indians and wolves and for olden-time princesses to stay in when they visited Iowa."

"Mmmmm. More likely a farmhouse," said Susan. "I don't think there are a lot of castles in Iowa, Em—"

"Actually, Susan," said Roy, "I don't think a farmhouse makes any more sense than a castle. It's too huge for a house. Plus, if it *were* part of a house, it'd have some windows in it, right? And maybe a door?"

They all looked up and agreed that the wall didn't have any windows in it, or doors either. Susan frowned.

"Maybe it was a really enormous barn?" Roy guessed. "But it doesn't matter much. The big question is, what can we do with it?"

The others agreed. Clearly, something so interesting and rare needed to be put to good use.

"I guess it could be a kind of fort," said Susan at last, "if we leaned some branches against it, maybe. But they'd have to be really long branches."

"And where would we get the branches from?" asked Roy, thinking practically. "Drag them from town?"

"Who cares!" said Henry impatiently. "We can figure out what to do with it later. In the meantime, we should claim it."

"Claim it?" asked Emma.

"Yeah, Em. Like when someone finds a planet or walks on the moon or something. Or back in pioneer days, when they staked out homesteads in the Wild West. It's *our* wall now. We found it, and we need to claim it before someone else does. Right, Roy?"

"We can if you want to." Roy nodded thoughtfully.

"Although *technically* it belongs to whoever owns this field."

Henry ignored this comment. Roy was his best friend and always had been, but sometimes it was necessary to ignore Roy in the name of fun. Henry wished his friend could understand that "technically" didn't always matter.

"But what are we going to claim it *with*?" Henry asked. "We should have a flag or a sign or something, a way to let people know that it's *our* wall. What have you guys got?"

They all emptied their pockets.

Henry had half a pack of very pungent bubble gum (the same gum that had left his hair a sticky mess), a handful of change, a crumpled dollar bill, the cell phone his mother made him carry, and a red rubber ball. Emma found one of the green handlebar tassels from her new bike (already pulled loose), a smiling-tooth sticker from the dentist's office, and another crumpled dollar bill. Susan found a tube of sparkle lip gloss, ten dollars (emergency money), a cell phone nobody ever had to remind her to carry, and a barrette. Roy found a funny-looking rock, a compass, and a mouse skull, which is not nearly as gross as it sounds. He pulled the skull out last, and it gleamed fragile and white in his hand.

"I don't know how we can make a sign or a flag with any of this stuff," said Henry, "but *that*"—he pointed at the skull—"gives me another idea. You know what would be awesome?" The others did not know, so Henry told them. "We should have some kind of ceremony. Make a sacrifice and say a prayer of thanks, like when shipwrecked people find a desert island. To thank the spirits of the field, or whatever, for letting us find the wall." Henry was excited. This would involve digging, jumping around, and make-believe: three of his favorite things.

Henry began to make a chanting noise that sounded like "Oh-ee-oh-ee," and bowed down to the wall. After a while, he turned and looked back at the others, wondering why nobody else had joined in his wordless song. They were all just watching him.

"A sacrifice?" Emma looked nervous.

Henry stopped chanting and sighed. "I don't mean a scary kind of sacrifice," he explained. "I mean a fun sacrifice."

"If we're going to do a sacrifice, we should do it right," said Susan. "A sacrifice should mean giving up something more than an old piece of bone." She eyed the skull with distaste. "A sacrifice should be something you care about. Something you want to keep. That's the *definition* of sacrifice, isn't it? That way, the spirits will know we're serious."

The others stared at her when she said the word "spirits." This didn't sound like the Susan they'd gotten used to over the last year, the Susan who ignored them and sometimes made fun of their games. This seemed more like the old Susan, and though they were delighted to welcome her return, they were all a little shocked.

She noticed them staring and stared right back, in a bug-eyed sort of way. "What?" she said. "I just mean— you know, if there *are* spirits."

Roy prodded her. "So, you think we need to give up something that matters to us?"

Susan nodded.

"Like . . . your cell phone?" asked Roy with a sneaky smile.

"Yeah," said Henry, smirking. "You sure do like *that*."

"No way," said Susan, putting it back in her pocket immediately. "Absolutely not. Mom and Dad would kill me."

"What about the money, then?" asked Emma.

Of all the things they were carrying with them, their money did seem like the only thing they had worth giving up, besides their two cell phones, which—everyone had to admit—they'd get skinned alive if they lost. It didn't seem likely that the spirits of the field would want a plastic tassel or some gum, so while Roy dug a hole at the base of the wall, Susan collected Emma and Henry's dollars.

"On second thought," Susan asked, holding up the money, "do you think just the two is enough? Plus the change? I feel bad giving the rest away, since it's not my money. It really belongs to Mom."

"Yeah, *sure,*" said Henry. "Just take *my* dollar and *Emma's* but keep your own money. *That* seems fair."

Despite Henry's grousing, they all agreed that two dollars should be plenty of sacrifice to gratify the spirits of the field, if there were such spirits. Last of all, Roy added the small white skull gently to the pile of money in the hole. It seemed right, since the mouse had likely been a field mouse. They all scrabbled the pile over with dirt.

When Henry's hand touched something hot and smooth, he jumped back. "Ow!" he yelped.

"What is it?" asked Emma.

Henry bent to pick up the hot something-or-other, then held it up so that they could all see. It was a large skeleton key the size of a teaspoon, so caked with dirt that none of them had noticed it lying camouflaged on the ground. Henry wiped it against his shirt, and as the dirt flaked off, everyone saw it was made of a bronzy kind of metal, with a rough surface and fancy scrollwork at the top.

"I guess it got hot in the sun and burned me," he said.

"Can I see it?" asked Roy.

"Sure," said Henry, handing it over. "But give it back. I want to keep it. It's mine."

Emma glanced at the key and then up at the wall. "Maybe it goes to the castle? It *looks* like a castle key."

Roy shook his head. "I don't think so. Whatever the wall used to be, even if it *was* a castle, it hasn't been in a long time. Any key to something so old would be long gone or buried deep underground by now." He handed the key back to Henry, who put it in his pocket.

"C'mon, guys," said Susan, bored with the key. "I'm thirsty. Let's think about heading back."

"But I want to finish the sacrifice," said Henry. He began to chant again and jump around.

"Fine." Susan relented. "But make it quick."

Henry jumped faster. He broke off a slender cornstalk and waved it above his head, chanting even louder. Then he stopped for a second to ask, "Hey, who wants to say the great appreciation prayer while I do my native corn dance of thanks?"

"I will!" piped up Emma, who began to pray loudly and with great feeling.

"Dear Wall, we think you are a very nice wall and we would like you to be our wall from now on. We hope two dollars and some cents is enough because the rest really belongs to Mrs. Levy and it's all we have. Thank you very much and we'll come see you again soon and maybe we'll bring you another present someday. Something better than a dead mouse. Okay? The End. AMEN!" She shouted this last word at the top of her lungs, and when she was done, Emma brushed her hands together and blew a kiss toward the little mound.

It wasn't quite the ceremonial prayer Henry had envisioned, but everyone (trying not to laugh) said "Amen" too. When it was over, they walked around the wall together (even Susan, who had forgotten she was thirsty), taking note of their gigantic new possession. It did, for all the silliness of the ceremony, make it feel official; it felt more theirs now that they'd claimed it. Ritual has that effect.

And that was when Emma said, "Roy?"

And Roy answered, "Yeah?"

And Emma pulled him over by the hand and pointed. "I know you said it's not the right key to the castle, but doesn't it *look* like the castle wants a key?"

Roy leaned down, looked at where Emma was pointing, and admitted she was right. There, about three feet from the ground, on the shady side of the wall, was a very dingy keyhole set into a metal plate. The metal plate was exactly the same bronzy color as the key.

"Hey, Henry, bring that key back over here a minute," he called.

Henry stuck his head around the corner of the wall. "Why?" He joined them.

"Just because," said Roy, who stood up, took the key, and fitted it into the hole.

"What's happening?" Susan asked, walking over to hover over her brother's shoulder.

"Henry's key seems to fit this keyhole," said Roy, "which is weird. Don't you think?" He joggled the key.

Henry squatted by the metal plate. "I've never seen a key fit into a *wall* before. Usually there's a door or something. I mean, there's nothing for this to open, right?"

"Yeah, but it *does* fit," said Roy. "I even think it'll turn." He held his breath as he turned it.

They all listened to the heavy grinding sound and the rough click that it made. They all waited, but nothing more happened. There didn't appear to be anything to actually unlock.

Roy gave the key back to Henry.

"Fascinating." Susan yawned. "Anyway," she said, "I think that since we've claimed the wall and it's one-fourth mine, I'm going to use it for a rest." She walked a few yards over and plunked right down beside their bikes. She combed out her hair with her fingers, applied a coat of lip gloss, wiped a smear of dirt from her right knee, and then plucked a thick blade of grass, which she placed between her thumbs. When she blew on it, it produced a wonderful piercing sound. One by one, the others followed her lead, until they were all lined up between the metal plate and the bikes, whistling on blades of grass (except for Emma, who could only make a thpbtttttt sound when she blew).

"Dang," said Henry, looking up at the wall leaning over them. "It's not so bad once you're out of the sun, but now that I'm not so hot, I'm thirsty."

"Join the club," said Susan.

"Yeah," said Roy. "We should really have brought some water with us." Roy was usually prepared.

"Ooh," said Susan. "Water! I wish I had a big cold glass of water right now, with a lot of crushed ice and a lemon."

"Or better yet—some pop!" said Roy.

"Or a slushy?" said Emma. "A cherry-lime one."

"Or a root beer float!" said Henry.

Which caused everyone to make the same sound at once—the sound you make when someone else is enjoying something yummy and they don't offer to share.

"Mmm," said Susan wistfully. "A root beer float would be perfect. I *sooo* wish we were at Annabelle's Diner right now."

Then—in the space of a breath, a moment—they *were* at Annabelle's!

They were lined up in exactly the same formation, sitting in a row against a wall, only now the wall was made of slick, smooth tile instead of rough dark stone. Instead of the summer heat, they breathed in chilly air scented with frying hamburgers. Instead of the cornfields, they looked up and saw a bustling room full of lunchtime diners and harried waitresses darting to and fro. Their bikes were there too, leaning against the wall beside them.

They all blinked. They all gasped. They all stared openmouthed at each other, but then a big voice boomed at them from above, from behind a cash register. "You kids know you can't bring them bikes in here. You better get 'em out fast. Before Annabelle sees ya. Now SCRAM!"

What else could they do? They scrammed! They hopped up and wheeled their bikes through the swinging doors that led to the street. They propped them up and sat down on a bench, stunned.

Finally Susan spoke. "What—just—happened?" she asked.

"No clue," said Henry.

Roy and Emma shrugged.

"Do you think anybody saw us?" asked Susan. "I mean, inside the diner. I mean, did they see us *appear?*"

"I don't *think* so," said Henry.

"It was loud and busy, and it's not the kind of place where people pay attention," explained Roy. "I guess."

At last Emma asked *the* question. "Was it . . . magic?"

Nobody answered her, so Emma tried again, a little louder. "I *said,* was it MAGIC?"

"It couldn't be, could it?!" said Susan. "Maybe it was an unexplained phenomenon, an optical illusion?" She spoke these words, but her face said something else. Her face, bright and flushed, said *Magic!*

"A what?" asked Emma.

Roy explained. "Susan means it's a kind of trick, Em. 'Illusion' is a word people use to explain things they can't figure out."

"But she doesn't mean it. Do you, Susan?" asked Henry.

"You really think this is magic, Roy?" asked Susan, turning to face him. "Actual magic?"

Roy pushed his bangs from his eyes and thought about this. "Like I said earlier, anything's possible. I don't know what we found, but I know we found something, and this feels like one time when thinking won't help. I have no idea what happened, but I'm not about to let this chance slip away. It wouldn't make any sense to waste it just because we don't *understand* it. Right?"

"Yeah!" said Henry excitedly. "Why not? What do we have to lose by trying?"

Emma bounced up and down on the bench beside him.

"Oh—my—gosh!" Susan was smiling broadly now, but then she bit her lip and added, "If any of you ever tell anyone else that I went along with this, that I *believed*—"

"What do you mean," asked Emma. "What's wrong with *believing*?"

Henry had another thought. "Of *course* I won't tell anyone. Jeez! In fact, *nobody* can, or it'll be ruined. That's, like, the first rule of magic, isn't it? In all the books when you find a magic talisman, you don't tell *anyone.* Magic *has* to stay a secret." He was very serious about this.

Emma, who was just beginning to discover such wonderful books as *Magic by the Lake,* nodded solemnly.

"Now everyone swear," Henry said. "Swear that you won't tell a soul." Henry looked at each of them one by one. "Swear!"

Susan swore quickly, with a giggle.

Emma's eyes were gigantic as she repeated after Susan. Sacrifices and swearing all in one day!

Roy appeared cool and thoughtful. "I solemnly swear," he said, "though I reserve the right to revisit this issue at a later time, since we just don't know what'll happen. Okay?"

Henry gave a brief head shake that meant "Yes, okay, sure, whatever you say, Roy" and also "That won't happen, goofball" before he went on in a rush of excitement. "And I swear too. Okay! Now, do you realize what we have? We have a *wishing wall*! We can wish anything we want! We can wish for wings and to fly, or we can wish for piles of money and then buy a baseball team, or we can wish ourselves right onto the moon, or . . . or . . . or . . . pirates!"

"And I can be a princess?" Emma was shivering with

excitement. The pale blond curls danced on top of her head.

"Sure!" said Henry. "As soon as we get back to that field, you can—"

"Now wait a minute," Susan cut in. "Even if it *is* magic and it's ours, I think it's too late to ride back there today. We'll miss dinner."

"What?" Henry yelped. "You're *nuts*! It's just a little after four o'clock right now, and we don't have to be home until the streetlights come on at six!"

Susan shook her head. "Think! By the time we get all the way out there, it will be nearly five, and we'll just have to turn around and come home again. There won't be any time for wishing at all, and I don't want to get home late and end up grounded. Then we won't be doing any wishing for at least a week!"

"Gah!" Henry was scornful of "thinking ahead," in general. As a rule, it ruined fun, but in this case, it felt like sheer madness.

"Besides," Susan said, ignoring him, "there's something else that has to happen first anyway."

"What, you want to call your mom and check in? You need to return your library books? You have to call Alexandria?" Henry asked in disbelief.

"No, you bonehead." Susan smiled. "What I *need*—

is to drink a delicious—frosty—frothy—creamy—scrumptious—root beer float! An icy beverage to sustain me for the arduous ride home. And since I happen to have ten dollars in my pocket, that's exactly what I'm going to do."

With a decided flounce, she got up from the bench, stuck out her tongue at Henry, turned sharply, and pushed her way through the swinging doors.

The others followed close behind, because Susan had ten dollars in her pocket and they did not, and also because, as even Henry had to admit, root beer floats are just another kind of magic.

working the wall

THE NEXT MORNING, Henry and Emma woke up early, raced through breakfast (Henry almost choked on a piece of too-dry rye toast), and began rummaging through the pantry shelves.

"What? Where on earth are you going?" sputtered their father through his coffee and his mustache as Emma and Henry ran from the kitchen, his newspaper fluttering in their wake.

"Aren't you even going to watch your cartoons?" called out their mom as they tore down the hall with granola bars spilling from their pockets. By the time she'd finished her sentence, the screen door was already slamming shut.

When they got to the yard, Emma and Henry found Susan and Roy cutting through the thick hedge that divided the two houses. They could make out arms, feet, and the shiny gleam of handlebars struggling through the thick foliage. Roy's head popped through, grinning from ear to ear. "Hey, guys," he said, pulling his body and bike into their yard and brushing off a few loose twigs. "We found a shortcut."

Roy was wearing his explorer uniform: khaki shorts and a matching shirt. Around his neck was a red bandanna. He appeared to be ready for a safari.

"Will there be tigers?" asked Emma faintly.

Susan, a few seconds behind her brother, pushed her way through the brambles with more than a few loud "oofs" and "ouches." She looked back at the mess of bent and broken branches, spit out a leaf, and crouched to retie a shoelace as she said, "More like we made a shortcut." But she straightened up and smiled as she continued. "Good deal that you guys aren't still sleeping. I was afraid we were going to have to wake you up."

"Ha! I bet we were up before you were," said Henry, folding his arms and waiting for Susan to finish pulling her bike through behind her. "We've been up forever. We would've been out sooner, but Mom and Dad made us eat breakfast."

"Ours too, which is totally unfair," grumped Susan. "It was just cold cereal. I mean, I would've been happy to wait for blueberry waffles or something—but raisin bran?"

"Let's GO!" shouted Emma.

About fourteen seconds later, they were on their bikes and moving fast, with their heads down and their eyes on the road before them. There was none of the previous day's singing, hollering, wheelie popping, or swerving. They barely took note of the traffic lights, much less the summer leaves rustling in the cool morning air. This was unfortunate, since it was a perfect morning for a bike ride: slightly damp, with a bright sun just beginning to make its way into the sky.

Periodically, Emma, who could not go quite so fast, would shout, "Hey, hey! Wait for meeee!" and the older kids would slow down so that she had a chance to catch up. But even so, in a short twenty minutes, they were back in the cornfields and rumbling down the rough dirt path.

Then, as if it were a ship on the ocean, the wall rose up slowly from the field, as it had the day before.

When they saw it, they sped up, but as each of them came close to the wall, they braked fast, planted their feet on the ground, and stared upward. First Susan stopped, then Henry, then Roy, and finally Emma—so that they stood in a line, each of them straddling their bike, each of them staring.

"What are we waiting for?" asked Henry. And since nobody had an answer, they got off their bikes (which toppled to the ground in a haphazard clatter) and made their way to the keyhole.

"Did you bring the key?" Susan asked Henry.

"What do you *think*?" said Henry.

Susan held out a hand and gestured. Her fingers said "Give it here."

Henry pulled the key from his pocket but did not pass it over. Instead, he polished it on his shirt, held it out before him, and admired the shine. He'd cleaned it with his mother's toothbrush the night before.

Susan stared him down. "Come on, Henry. Let me have it," she said. "Everyone else, line up and put a hand on the wall!"

Henry was unmoved. "It's still my key," he said, "and anyway, how do you even know we have to be *touching* the wall? Maybe we just have to be near it."

"Do you want to try *not* touching the wall and see what happens?" said Susan. "The rest of us will tell you all about our adventure when we get back."

Roy sighed. "I think you two are going to have to learn to take turns being bossy. I'm not sure we have room in this adventure for an oldest brother and an oldest sister too."

It should be explained that Henry and Susan weren't really fighting. For ten years, they had been tussling this way, ever since two-year-old Susan had first tried to fit baby Henry into her pink doll bed.

"Well, *someone* needs to turn it," Susan said to her brother. "He's wasting time."

"But *I* found the key," Henry insisted.

"Yes, but I'm the oldest," Susan said, planting her hands on her hips.

Henry planted his hands on his hips and did a pretty fair imitation of Susan, wiggling his head on his shoulders and flipping an imaginary head of hair. "And *I'm* the one holding the key. Anyway, Roy got to turn the key yesterday, and you made the wish for the root beer floats, so it's only fair that I take a turn today. Or Emma," he added generously.

Emma shook her head wordlessly at that suggestion. She didn't want to go first. She *never* went first. She wouldn't know how.

"Fine." Susan relented in the name of speeding things along. "Fine, but let's go! What are we wishing for? Magic awaits!"

So Henry turned the key until they all heard the satisfying click, and he shouted out fiercely, in his best pirate voice, "Arrrrrrr! Pirates! I wish we were pirates!"

There was a deep moment of silence. A breezeless, birdless, wondrous moment of nothing.

And then . . .

Nothing happened.

Nobody turned into a pirate. Nobody saw a pirate carousing off in the distance. There wasn't even a salty breath of sea spray wafting around them or the faint odor of rum casks and unwashed sailors lingering in the air. Nothing!

Henry's face fell.

Susan said, "Okay. You made your wish. It's my turn." She held out her hand again for the key.

But Henry looked so disappointed that she withdrew her upturned palm. "Sorry," she said. "Maybe we just need to wait a minute so that the magic has a chance to warm up."

Henry kicked at the dirt. "Or maybe it was just a one-time thing, a fluke, and we wasted it on root beer floats. Man!"

"You really think so?" asked Susan.

Henry sulked and nodded.

"I suppose it's *possible* that it was a one-time thing," Roy offered. "Who really knows? But before we get too frustrated, let's try to figure it out. Isolate our variables."

"What's that mean?" asked Emma. "It sounds ouchy."

"It's not a bad thing, Em. It just means we should figure out precisely what we're doing, like in a science experiment. See, it doesn't have to be all or nothing. There might just be tricks to the magic. The way we turn the key, for instance. Maybe you don't have to turn the key every time you make a wish. Maybe it's more like a light switch and it stays the way you leave it, either on or off."

"Huh?" Now Emma was *really* confused.

Roy explained. "See, yesterday, we turned the key, and the magic happened, so we assumed that we activated the wall by turning the key. If that were the case, it would make sense that we'd need to activate it every time we wanted to use it, whenever we wanted a wish. But if it *isn't* like that, if it's like an on-and-off switch, or a lock . . ."

"That's *just* what it is!" shouted Henry, looking up. "A lock! The whole wall is kind of like a giant lock, right?"

Roy looked excited. "Sure! In which case, when we turned it yesterday, we *unlocked* it, but when we turned it today, we *locked* it again!"

"Oh!" said Emma, beginning to understand. "We left it unlocked overnight?"

"Exactly!" said Roy. "So now we just need to turn it again."

Susan beamed at her brother. "You know, as little brothers go, you're pretty smart!"

Hopeful again, Henry nodded, then crouched back down to the keyhole and turned the key. This time, he spoke respectfully, even carefully. He didn't sound like himself at all when he said, "Please, wall, we'd very much like to wish for a pirate adventure, if that's okay with you."

And this time . . .

Nothing happened *again*!

"I guess I was wrong," Roy apologized sheepishly. "Try turning it back the other way?"

"ARRGHHH!" Henry yelled, sounding even more like a pirate, but now by accident.

Susan began to say, "Maybe we just need to wait for—" But before she could finish her sentence, Henry kicked the wall.

"Don't kick it!" Emma got upset. "Poor wall. You'll make him angry."

Henry kicked it again. "I don't CARE! Darn wall—"

"Maybe," Susan said, "maybe there's another variable? Like, maybe the problem isn't the wall but the wish. Maybe the wall just doesn't like pirates, and you should try wishing for something else."

Henry thought about this and nodded. "Yeah. Yeah,

okay, that's possible. I'll try." He took a deep breath. Then, touching the wall lightly with the fingers of one hand, Henry said, "I wish I could fly." After that, he stepped away from the wall and flapped his arms. He flapped them tentatively at first, and then harder, but other than fanning Emma's face a bit, nothing seemed to be any different.

"Maybe you need a running start?" suggested Susan.

Henry tried that too, hurtling forward and launching himself very briefly over the tips of the young cornstalks, but then his sneakers hit the ground again, hard.

Susan and Roy couldn't help looking disappointed. Emma, who had been holding her breath, let it out in a gust.

"Aw, man," Henry said in a thoroughly frustrated tone. "It just isn't working."

And everyone had to admit that it really *didn't* seem to be working. None of them wanted to admit defeat, but they all (with the possible exception of Emma) felt a little silly standing for so long with their hands on the wall, which they'd been doing since before the first pirate wish. One by one, they sat down a few feet away, beside their scattered bikes. First Susan, then Roy, and finally Emma.

All except Henry. Henry just stared at the wall, his

teeth clenched, his hands balled into fists. He refused to be beaten, though the wall was proving a worthy adversary. He bellowed again and kicked the wall even harder. He mumbled some words he wasn't supposed to say (words *you* certainly aren't supposed to say) under his breath, kicked the wall a third time, mumbled another something, and turned beet red.

Nobody was paying much attention to Henry by this point. Instead, they busied themselves with munching their emergency granola bars. Roy, who had cleverly rubber-banded a water bottle to his bike's frame, took a swig and passed the bottle. Who needs

supplies for an adventure that isn't going to happen?

But it's too bad they were distracted, because the next second, as Henry kicked the wall a fourth time and said, "Aw, this is a waste of time. I wish I was at the CineSix instead—"

He disappeared!

The others didn't. Sprawled in the scrabbly grass with their bikes, they were completely unprepared for Henry's instantaneous departure. Emma saw him blink away out of the corner of her eye and shrieked. Susan's jaw dropped, and a big mouthful of water spilled out onto her shorts. Roy threw down a handful of trail mix, jumped up, and ran to the wall, but not quickly enough.

Susan and Emma scrambled after him, and because they were all scared to have lost Henry, they quickly touched the wall and shouted at the same time, as if they had rehearsed for this moment, "The CineSix!"

Suddenly they were at the movies! Surrounding them was the scent of stale popcorn and the soft darkness of a completely empty theater.

Thank goodness the magic was feeling kind and blinked them to the same spot it had blinked Henry to. It didn't have to do this, since the Quiet Falls CineSix offers (as you might imagine) six fabulous screens, and the magic could just as easily have dropped Susan, Roy, and Emma in a different room. If it were feeling truly ornery, the wall could have chosen to send them to a different CineSix altogether, a movie theater in Baltimore or Boise. But the magic was generous and blinked them gently into the same theater as Henry. They found themselves facing the back of the room, with their hands against a carpeted wall. They turned around to face the screen, and found Henry a few feet away, looking grumpy. Even in the dark, they could see his crossed arms and cranky expression.

"This doesn't count as my wish," he said in a surly tone. "I never would have wasted a wish on the movies. Plus, if I *were* going to wish for a movie, it wouldn't be *this* one. Ugh. Look!" He uncrossed his arms and pointed.

On the huge screen, a woman and a man were kissing loudly in the woods. The woman was wearing scant rags and the man looked terribly pained. He clutched one of his legs in such a way that suggested the leg was broken, but he kept on kissing the woman through his utmost agony and her lustrous hair, which kept getting in both their eyes. Near the couple was a crashed airplane.

The four kids stared. Henry wore a look of true revulsion and Roy one of disinterest. Susan couldn't help blushing. Only Emma was curious.

"Why are they kissing when he's hurt?" she asked. She looked to Susan for an answer. "Why doesn't she go get help? Why doesn't he lie down and get some rest?"

"Who cares!" said Henry, louder than he meant to. "Why is this even *playing*? Shouldn't this place be all locked up? The matinee shouldn't start for hours yet."

"Maybe," whispered Susan cautiously, "there's someone here, watching it. Someone who works here." She glanced around, but there didn't seem to be anyone else in the theater.

"Let's go," said Henry.

They all made for the brightly glowing EXIT sign beneath the screen, and nobody spoke, but when Susan's hand pushed open the door, a terrible alarm sounded, and they all ran as fast as they could. They bolted onto the sidewalk and ran straight for a row of hedges beside the building, where they huddled, hiding until it became clear nobody was coming.

"Not exactly tight security, huh?" asked Henry, standing up and looking around.

"Well, have you seen the kids who work here?" said Roy. "They all look half-asleep most of the time. We could probably watch the whole movie and nobody would even notice." But nobody thought that sounded like much fun.

Once they felt safe in the open, the kids prepared to head back to the field, until it dawned on them that they did not have their bikes. "I guess they weren't touching the wall this time," said Roy, smacking himself in the head and remembering the clatter the bikes had made falling to the ground.

Henry groaned at the thought of walking all the way back to the wall. "It'll take us forever to get there, an hour at least," he said, sitting down on the curb, exhausted by the very thought.

"Yeah," said Susan, "it will, but maybe while we walk, we can figure out what we're doing wrong. I mean, why won't the wall work when we *mean* for it to? Is it a trick? Is *that* the secret of the wall? That it only does accidental magic?"

Roy answered her. "How could the wall possibly know whether we've planned a wish or not?"

"Magic knows stuff," said Emma, sounding very certain. "It just does."

"I think the magic is being mean!" said Henry, standing back up. "I bet it could let us do whatever we want, only it doesn't want to. It's messing with us."

"No." Roy thought for a minute. "I really don't think that's it. I still think there are rules, and we're wishing wrong."

"What do you mean?" asked Susan. "You mean like the wish has to be a good deed or something? Boy Scout magic?" She pointed to Roy's tan uniform.

"No," he said, "because root beer floats aren't exactly what you'd call good deeds." He adjusted his bandanna and added, "And for your information, I'm *not* a Boy Scout. I'm an explorer."

"Let's think," said Susan. "What've we wished for so far?"

"An adventure with pirates," said Henry, "and the ability to fly. But we haven't gotten either of those wishes. The magic's only happened twice, and both times that it's worked, we were wishing for something dumb."

"Not dumb," said Susan. "Just regular. Root beer floats. Movies."

Everyone thought about this for a minute.

"Huh," said Roy, "I wonder if that's it. I wonder if it's only normal stuff the wall can give us. Maybe, instead of wishing for a big thing like flying, we should be wishing for something smaller. Something—"

"Boring?" suggested Henry, making a sour face. "How about soup? You want to wish for some soup? Or maybe we should wish for a newspaper, or a chance to clean out the basement."

But Emma, who had been listening quietly, shook her head and said, "But we *didn't* wish for root beer floats. We didn't wish for movies either."

"What's that, Em?" asked Susan.

"We didn't," said Emma. "We didn't wish for ice cream or movies. We wished to be at the CineSix and at Annabelle's Diner."

"We did?" Roy scratched his ear and tried to remember.

"Emma's right," said Susan. "We all were *thinking* about root beer floats, but that wasn't what I said. What I *said* was that I wanted to *be at Annabelle's.*"

"That's true," said Roy. "And today, we wished to be at the CineSix. Both times that the magic worked, someone was wishing to be in a different *place.*"

"A different *place,*" echoed Emma.

"That makes sense!" Susan burst out. "Tons of sense. It's a *wall,* after all. And a wall is a *place.* Maybe it's like that book Emma just read, *Magic by the Lake.* Remember that? How they have to wish watery wishes because the magic is watery magic. Since this is a wall, maybe we have to wish wall-ish wishes."

Roy nodded. "Right . . . okay . . . then maybe the wall isn't a magic talisman, exactly. Maybe it doesn't grant wishes, so much as it can become a different wall."

Emma was struggling to understand. "So, we have to turn on the wall, and then when it's *on,* it can change into other walls—any other wall we want—and it can take us with it?"

"I think so," said Roy excitedly.

"If I'd gotten to wish to be in a castle today, instead of Henry wishing for pirates, it would have worked?" asked Emma.

"Maybe," said Roy. "Maybe so."

They all thought about this, and it did seem to make sense, so they were all feeling hopeful again when they stopped by Roy and Susan's house to get a quick lunch before the long walk back to the wall.

Unfortunately, they weren't counting on Mr. Levy being home, which he was. This was something that happened from time to time because he was a college professor and had what he called "flexibility." His flexibility came in handy when Roy had chicken pox and had to stay home from school, but sometimes it was a pain. Like now.

"How about a treat, gang?" he called out through the screen door as they walked up the steps of the front porch. "My committee meeting got canceled, so I thought I'd play hooky and take you all to the movies! Yay!"

The kids paused, each counting on someone else to

dream up a good excuse. When nobody did, there was really no way they could turn down a trip to the movies without letting Mr. Levy know that something fishy was going on. Roy tried his best, saying, "The early show doesn't start for an hour or two, Dad."

"I know!" Mr. Levy smacked his hands together. "That's why I thought we'd go get an early lunch first! I thought we'd go to the Hot Dog Shack! For footlongs and slaw! How's that sound? Yeah!"

Susan couldn't see any way around spending the afternoon with her very generous and boisterous father. She sighed, "I *guess* so." And the others agreed.

Mr. Levy had no idea why the kids all seemed so downhearted at a surprise trip to the movies, but he tried in vain to fire them up. "Maybe I'll buy ice cream after? Wouldn't that be cool? Don't tell your mom."

"That'd be great, Dad," said Roy, trying to sound excited but not really succeeding.

"Woo hoo?" Mr. Levy looked puzzled.

"Woo," said Susan as she climbed into the car, "hoo."

As he drove, Mr. Levy shook his head. "You kids today sure are spoiled. Why, back when I was a boy, I would've loved a trip to the movies. And hot dogs? And ice cream? I would've been over the moon!"

Although nobody was exactly over the moon at the

thought of another afternoon without magic, when they saw that there was a good movie starting at just the right time (a swashbuckling adventure about a pirate princess), it wasn't *so* terrible, and they *did* manage to eat a large banana split with extra marshmallow sauce, for Mr. Levy's sake. It was *very* gracious of them.

And the marshmallow helped to ease the pain— the terrible pain of knowing that the day was pretty much shot and that they'd have to wait yet another day to see if they were right about the magic.

Magic in the Night

BACK AT HOME an hour before dinner, the kids were sticky-faced and decidedly unhungry. In fact, all of them felt faintly sick, so they headed for the back porch of the Levy house, which was screened in and a nice place to be when the mosquitoes came out.

Everyone found a good sprawling spot and settled in to rest. Susan took up residence on a white wicker couch, Henry fell into a beanbag, Emma eased herself into an aging Adirondack chair, and Roy found himself a particularly nice lying-down spot under the coffee table. They all sipped cool glasses of water and rested.

After a bit, Henry raised his head. "Hey, Roy, do you think we could eat dinner here tonight?"

"Ugh," Susan moaned. "How can you be thinking of *food*?"

"I'm not!" Henry insisted. "Just the opposite. I figure

our mom will make us clean our plates if we go home, and your parents won't, because we'll be guests and all. Also, tonight is tuna noodle casserole at our house."

Susan thought about tuna noodle casserole, groaned in sympathy, and yelled over one shoulder and into the house, "Mo-oooom? Mom! Can Henry and Emma stay for dinner?"

None of the kids could make out the garbled response that came echoing back through the house, but it had the tone of yes.

Henry gave Emma a poke in the ribs, tickled her so that she gave a giggle and slid onto the floor. "Hey, Emma," he said. "Run next door and see if it's cool with Mom and Dad."

Emma, a tangle of legs and arms on the floor, looked up at her brother and frowned. "Why should I? Why can't *you* go? You always make me do stuff." Emma's tight tummy had turned her obstinate.

"Because," he said.

"Because *why?*"

Henry thought for a minute. "Because you're tiny and cute, and people like to say yes to you."

Emma considered this idea. She hadn't realized that it was true, but if it was, it had distinct possibilities. "If I do, can I make the next wish?"

Henry looked over at Susan and Roy, who both nodded at Emma. Susan waved a limp, tired hand that said "Sure. Sure. I'm too stuffed to care."

Emma, thinking she might want to be obstinate more often, walked next door to ask for permission and came back to tell everyone that Dad had said, "For Pete's sake! Why didn't you ask before I snapped these beans?" Which meant "Okay, okay."

Emma slid into her chair again but found she didn't feel quite as tired as before. "Can we go *soon?*" she asked, swinging her legs. "For my wish? Can we?"

"First thing in the morning," Henry said, slumping deeper into his beanbag and closing his eyes.

"No," she said. "I mean tonight! Can we go tonight?"

"Tonight?" Roy sat up and slid from under the coffee table, bonking his head slightly. "Does it work at night? In the books, kids always wait until morning to make the next wish. One wish a day. Right?"

"Yeah," said Susan, pushing herself awkwardly to an upright position. "Maybe because *those* kids weren't supposed to go running around after dark any more than *we* are."

"Maybe the wall would let us," said Emma. "All our wishes so far have been itsy-bitsy ones."

"She's got a point," said Henry, "and maybe the

kids in the books were just dumb. Maybe they could have been magic-ing all night long and they just didn't realize it."

"Or maybe," said Susan, "they just didn't like to get in trouble. Do you guys know what my mom will do to me if I lead the three of you out into the fields at midnight?"

Henry dismissed this with a wave of his hand. "Then you don't have to come," he said, "but you can't stop us from trying."

"In that case, I *better* come," said Susan. "Who knows what trouble you kids will get into if I'm *not* there."

With that decided, everyone fell silent, thinking about the nighttime adventure that lay in wait. A little later, Mrs. Levy called them in to dinner, which turned out to be barbecued chicken and corn on the cob dripping with butter, so everyone managed to eat more than expected, despite their marshy and mallowy stomachs.

After dinner, they assembled in the Levys' downstairs bathroom, locked the door, perched on the rim of the bathtub, and in hushed tones discussed their plans, which were greatly complicated by the fact that without their bikes, they were going to have to walk to the wall in what Emma referred to with a shiver as "the darkest dark of night." They agreed to meet as soon as their parents went to sleep.

Although their plan was thrilling, it was also imprecise. Henry and Emma's parents turned in early because they had to open up the pharmacy at seven o'clock in the morning, while Susan and Roy's parents stayed up late playing a card game in the kitchen. As a result, Emma and Henry found themselves itchy in the bushes, watching for the lights to go off at the Levy house. For distraction, they busied themselves with slapping at the bugs (real and imagined) that landed on their arms and legs and playing Twenty Questions, which was no fun for Henry since Emma only thought of characters from fairy tales, so Henry always won.

Finally Susan and Roy emerged from their house. Bathed in thin moonlight, the kids set off walking and alternately running as fast as they could toward the cornfields. They were in a hurry, but not in too big a hurry to be thrilled by the experience of running at midnight. The darkness felt like a disguise, and the streets resembled old movie sets in the yellow lamplight. Not a single car passed them as they ran (as though the magic had somehow put everyone else in the world to sleep), and most of the windows they passed were dark and full of sheer blowing curtains. It was kind of spooky, with the trees casting strange shadows on the deserted sidewalks, but it was a good kind of spooky. Nothing seemed quite real. There were bats above and scuttling noises in the gutters that might have been leaves or bugs or—

"Gosh, this is cool," said Henry in the dim light.

"Like a mission," said Roy. "Top-secret."

"It really is," said Susan. "I haven't had this much fun in forever," she laughed. "Not since—"

"Since what?" asked Emma.

But Susan had already run on ahead, so Emma followed.

With their feet pounding a steady rhythm on the asphalt, they sped along in the moonlight, but when their sneakers hit gravel and they left the streetlights behind them and cut into the corn, the moon ducked behind a cloud and disappeared. They all gasped into the darkness, their faces lit only by the greenish blinking of a million fireflies. It was breathtaking, mesmerizing, and as the fireflies began to blink in unison, the kids stopped to stare. All around them, the greenish light from the bugs pulsed like a dream. Was this really happening? Was every night like this—this magical? Why did anyone ever go to bed?

The corn rustled, a faint breeze wafted past them,

and things buzzed everywhere in the velvet darkness. With no way to see the ground ahead or gauge the distance they'd already traveled, the kids tried hard to stay on the path and trusted that the wall was somewhere ahead. They trusted, and despite the tricky terrain, they arrived just as the moon reappeared, bringing visibility with it.

The scattered bikes gleamed in the silvery light. Everyone felt jittery. The dark, fast run had been an adventure of its own, and if anything, they were more excited about the magic than before.

"You ready, Em?" asked Roy.

"I think so," she said. "I want to wish for Merlin's castle. Is that an okay wish? Will it work? It's got walls in it, right?"

"Merlin's castle?" Henry asked. "Camelot? Awesome!"

"Really, Em?" Susan said. "You don't want princesses?"

"Well," said Emma, thinking, "I do, but I don't actually *know* any real princesses, just Cinderella and Sleeping Beauty and stuff. Roy and Henry said that it needs to be a *real* building instead of make-believe, so I thought of Merlin because Merlin's castle was real. I know it's real because I saw it on the History Channel."

Susan managed to restrain a giggle. "Maybe," she said. "Anyway, you can try."

"Besides," added Emma practically, "if it's a castle, you never know. There might be an extra princess hanging around."

Susan let out her giggle, but it turned out to be a friendly chuckle and not a snarky snicker. She smiled warmly at Emma. "Anything's possible, Em, but I suppose we won't know for sure until you wish." She set her hand on Emma's shoulder and looked around at her friends. "Is everyone touching the wall? Henry, you've got the key? Do we need to turn it again?"

Henry fitted the key into the lock and turned it until it made a satisfying clicking noise. Emma took a deep, deep breath and, glancing around at the others for support, she squeaked excitedly, "I wish you would turn into Merlin's castle, Mister Wall!"

And then . . .

It happened!

Suddenly they were touching a new wall, a different wall, a rounded wall in an empty room. There was a single square window, and together, the kids gathered to peer out over a dark land full of shadows. Under a half-moon, the world glittered like ice. Henry, Emma, Susan, and Roy could just make out a forest of very tall trees, their branches tangled against the sky.

"Yeah!" shouted Henry.

They all beamed, thrilled at finally having wished correctly, but then the gloom of the empty round room descended on them.

"*This* is a castle?" asked Emma. "Really? It's not like I pictured it at all. Where's the stained glass? Where's the jester? Where are all the servants? Nobody's dancing—"

"I guess this is the *real* Camelot," said Susan, looking at the empty fields beyond the trees. When she stepped away from the sill, her hands were gritty. She wiped them on her shorts and said, "What a weird room. I think we must be in a tower of some kind. It's pretty dirty, whatever it is."

"Who cares?" Henry shouted, jumping from foot to foot. "Who cares how dirty it is? It worked! The magic worked! Even if this is the crummiest castle in the universe, we finally, *finally* figured out the magic!"

This was true, so they all, even Emma in her jester-less chagrin, ignored the chill and the smell and rejoiced instead. Henry and Roy high-fived, while Susan spun in a circle and Emma did a giddy dance for joy that made her look as though she'd rolled in an anthill and was now very itchy. Then they headed—excitedly, hurriedly—out into the stone staircase beyond the round room.

Shivering, they crept slowly and carefully down, down, down the cold spiral staircase for what felt like a long time, alert and watching for adventure. When the staircase ended, Henry, Emma, Susan, and Roy found themselves in yet another stone room, a kind of foyer, considerably larger, with six doorways leading off in different directions. Somehow, the ominous darkness beyond *those* openings seemed worse than the ominous darkness in the staircase they'd come from.

The room in which they now stood was at least more interesting than the round room they'd arrived in. Besides the doorways, there were jagged-looking spears decorating the walls and a row of small high windows letting in sharp rays of moonlight. Below the windows, in the one wall devoid of ominous dark doorways, stood a massive wooden door covered in spikes and rusty hinges. Roy went up for a closer inspection and found a kind of leather door pull, but when he tugged on it, the door didn't budge.

It took all of them heaving and huffing and pushing, but finally the door swung open and they burst out into the moonlight, into a muddy, weedy yard surrounded by more stone walls. There was stone on every side.

"They sure like stone here," said Henry, slapping a hand against a wall. "I wonder how long it took to build this castle. I mean, it's not like they have cranes and bulldozers."

"Probably they have servants or serfs to lug the stones around instead," Roy said.

Emma felt her sneakers sinking into the mud. She pulled them out and tried to scrape them clean on a fallen branch. "Can I maybe have a different wish?" she asked, wrinkling her nose. "Can I try again? It's stinky here."

"Not tonight," said Henry, "but eventually, after the rest of us have had a turn. And yeah, it *is* stinky here."

"Kind of caveman-ish too." Susan nudged at a stray bone lying on the ground with her foot and wondered what kind of bone it was. "I thought it'd be less Neanderthal and more . . . I don't know . . . purple and silver."

They all stared at the bone, then up at the thick walls around the courtyard, which were impossibly thick and about twenty feet high.

"I guess they're to keep people out, not just in," Susan suggested.

"I don't know," said Henry, "but they're way too high to climb. That's for sure."

In one corner of the yard, pigs slumbered noisily

in a great pile. One wakeful beast rooted in the dirt, though for what, nobody wanted to guess. Susan kicked the bone in the direction of the pigs and they stirred.

Although the courtyard was a dismal, dingy, odorous place and the kids were freezing in the dank midnight air, the moon and the stars above the walls glittered with a special light. They looked somehow close to the ground, as though they were hanging just over the walls.

Everyone gazed up, but after they had taken note of the stars and the moon (and the snoring and snorting swine), there wasn't much to do, and they stood around, waiting for an adventure to happen to them. Henry inspected a broken wheelbarrow of sorts, and Susan stepped in a greenish puddle and pulled her foot out with a slurp. The slurp made the bad odor stronger.

Finally, after nine minutes that felt like ninety, Emma stomped a foot and asked, "Where *is* everyone?"

"Asleep, I guess," replied Roy. "After all, it's nighttime." He yawned, as if on cue.

"You mean, I won't get to see *anyone*?" asked Emma, sounding despondent and maybe a little overtired.

"Not unless someone's having a nightmare or getting a midnight snack," said Henry. "Man! Having magical adventures isn't as fun as I thought it'd be. Let's just go home."

But just as he said this, they all heard a funny sound, a hacking cough. It came from a low building (if you could call it a building) off to the right, a building they hadn't noticed in the shadows. It was really just a small lean-to, a series of wooden planks propped against one of the stone walls of the yard. There was a dark hole of a doorway, and a faint glimmer came from within.

The kids all froze.

The coughing was followed by a mumble of funny words. Something like "deednir evelcyre vera uoysiht gnid aerera uoyfi."

"Maybe," whispered Emma, "maybe we *should* go home. I won't mind. I won't need another wish or anything."

But Henry was already moving toward the door, so the others followed. Creeping closer, they saw a flicker and a wisp of smoke rising in the moonlight through the doorway in the lean-to. The others kept at a distance, but Henry went and stood a few feet from the doorway. "*Someone's* awake, at least," he whispered, "but listen to him—he's either totally crazy or he doesn't speak any English."

"Or both," added Roy.

"Maybe he's contagious too," murmured Susan warily.

"Jeez," said Henry. "Now is *not* the time to worry about germs."

Susan had already moved on to other concerns. "Do you think the magic doesn't translate for us?" she whispered.

"What do you mean?" asked Roy quietly.

"I never thought about it before," she whispered, "but you know how in books, kids who time-travel can always understand people in other countries, and in the past and stuff? Well, maybe our magic doesn't do that, and if it doesn't, we won't be able to understand anything anyone says anywhere we go, which would be *awful*."

"You've got a point," said Henry, craning his neck to see inside the hovel. "But wouldn't they speak English in Camelot? It's in England!"

Perhaps he spoke too loudly, because just then a man burst through the smoky doorway—a wild-eyed man with a rat sitting on his shoulder. The man stared at Henry, and Henry stared back. The rat, who was missing half of its tail, stared too.

"Hargh!" spat the man, coughing and hacking. The rat crawled up into the man's beard, maybe to avoid

getting wet. "Hargh!" coughed the man. He wore a dirty brown tunic. There were twigs and what looked to be a bird's nest tangled in his long, matted hair, and his face was caked with mud. He was missing a number of teeth, and in one hand, he held a long, dark knife. It glinted in the moonlight.

Roy froze.

Emma squeaked.

Susan turned to run.

But Henry was stuck, close enough to smell the man (who did not smell as bad as you might think, given his dismal appearance—rather like a pile of old leaves). Henry felt a hand close on his shoulder. His stomach flipped.

"Hargh!" The man coughed again and dry leaves flew from his ragged cloak onto the ground. Then he said, "Come!"

Henry was paralyzed.

The man cleared his throat, stood up perfectly straight, and said, in very proper English such as a grown-up actor might use in a very serious movie, "Please come, I haven't time to wait." Although his voice was pleasant, he was frightening to look at, running his tongue over his three visible teeth.

Then Henry felt the man's fingers like a claw on his

arm, but he still did not move. His mind churned.

"Hello?" the man asked, shaking Henry's arm roughly. "Hello? Are you deaf?"

"No!" called out Emma. "He's not!"

"Then all of you come NOW!" said the man, releasing Henry and turning to go back into his hovel. "*Follow* me, I say!" But when he looked back over his shoulder and saw all four kids still frozen in their tracks, he threw his knife emphatically to the ground. "Oh, this just won't do!" he said. "What is *wrong* with the children of the future? Don't they listen to their elders?"

With a quick movement that caused the rat to tumble from his shoulder, the filthy man strode back over and grabbed hold of Henry's arm again. "I said COME!" he shouted as he dragged Henry, stumbling and shocked, through the dark doorway.

Greetings and Glimpses

THE ADVENTURE had taken hold of Henry, so now Susan, Roy, and Emma took hold of the adventure! Susan arrived at the lean-to first and ducked inside, with the others close on her heels. In the odd dim light of the lean-to, they found Henry sitting in the corner on a lumpy pile of leaves and blankets.

Henry jumped up when they entered, but the strange man blocked the doorway. He stood in the very center of the room, at a small table that was covered with herbs and leaves. A blue fire burned in a metal bowl before him. The filthy old fellow did not appear to be concerned with the entrance of Susan, Roy, and Emma behind him. He was chopping something and tossing bits into the bowl.

"Fingers?" whispered Emma to Susan beside her. Susan did not reply.

Nobody wanted to anger the man, but he was busy, distracted for now—and they couldn't just stay put, could they? Henry looked up at the others and mouthed something, but it didn't matter what he was trying to say because before anyone could act, the strange man spoke.

"What are you called?" he said as he poured a trickle of water into the chopped fingers (or whatever they were) and stirred the mess together. "Your names. What are they?" He used a courteous tone, as though he had not just grabbed at Henry, as though he were not a filthy madman.

Susan felt Emma's cold hand creep into hers and she remembered that she was the oldest, so she stepped forward, on best behavior. She cleared her throat and said, "Pardon me, sir?"

"You have names, don't you? What are they? I knew to expect four children—my visions told me you'd be arriving—but I don't know your names." The filthy man turned around and handed Roy, Susan, and Emma each a dish full of chopped-up stuff, which only looked like soupy weeds and sticks, and not fingers after all. "My visions can be weak on details. You know how it is with visions."

When he leaned down to hand Emma her bowl, he

winked, which made him seem friendly. Emma tried to wink back but only succeeded in squinting both eyes. The man chuckled. "What should I call you?" he asked, a smile lingering in a corner of his mouth.

"Emma," said Emma timidly. "Or something else if you want."

The man stepped back to look her up and down. He said, "No. Emma is fine. Suits you."

Feeling bolder, but still speaking softly, Emma confessed, "Actually, my name is Emily, Emily Rose O'Dell, but nobody calls me Emily because there are four Emilys in my class at school. It's a very popular name."

"Why then, Emma is perfect," said the man, "a great name!" He smiled, showing Emma his three teeth.

For some reason, saying the word "great" made the man seem harmless, because nobody can smile and say "great" and still seem evil—even if they happen to be a filthy old man who smells like musty leaves and has three teeth and a terrible cough. Villains never think things are great, not even their own dastardly plots. Now the filthy old man seemed friendly, grinning gummily down at them, waiting for their names. The kids looked into their bowls. Were they supposed to drink it?

Susan thought maybe she could just pretend to sip

it, to be polite. "My name is Susan," said Susan, starting to raise the shallow bowl to her lips.

"No!" cried the man. "Don't!"

She lowered it again fast, sloshing as she did so. "I'm sorry. I thought—why? Is it poison?"

The man barked a funny cough-laugh into his matted beard. "Hargh! Ha-ha-haw! No, no, it won't hurt you, but it'll taste like a moldy shoe."

Susan sniffed the bowl and discovered that it did smell something like a shoe.

"Besides, I don't have time to make more, so let's not waste it." He turned back to Henry and shoved a dish into his hands too. Henry cautiously edged around the table and rejoined the others.

"What is it?" Susan peered into the dish.

"First things first, Susan. I need all your names," said the man insistently. "It's only proper."

So Henry and Roy told him their names too.

The man nodded at them. "Good, good."

Then Roy asked, "What about you, sir? What's your name?"

"Why, don't you know? After all, it was your wish that brought us together."

"It was my wish," said Emma proudly.

"Well, then you should know," said the man,

patting her head. "Naturally, I'm Merlin."

Henry, Emma, Susan, and Roy, who had been expecting a wise-looking wizard with a wand, a long white beard, and maybe a blue cone-shaped hat, were surprised.

"I didn't think—" began Emma.

"That's very dangerous," said Merlin, shaking his head from side to side, "not thinking."

Henry brushed the leaves from his shorts, now that all signs of danger had passed, and said grumpily, "I thought Merlin was supposed to be a good guy. If you're Merlin, why'd you grab me like that?" He rubbed his arm, which was sore where Merlin had gripped him.

"Yes, I am sorry about that, but I couldn't have you all out there waking people up, and my potion was burning, so I couldn't afford to stand and chitchat all night either. When you wouldn't come with me, it seemed the only way to get you all inside."

"You should have just asked us nicely," said Susan. "Why on earth would you come to the door with a knife?"

"Because I was in the middle of chopping," said Merlin, "which generally requires a knife. And if you'll recall, I did ask nicely, but people never seem to respond well when I ask nicely." He wiped a clump of what appeared to be dried bird poop from his hair as he said, "For some reason, magical visitors are always nervous around me at first."

"I can't imagine why," said Susan. She wondered how long the poop had been there.

"Do you get lots of magical visitors?" asked Henry, deciding that he'd rather be friends with Merlin than not.

"Yes," answered Merlin proudly. "I'm quite famous in certain circles. There are movies about me, and statues, plus I'm in loads of books. I even got a mention in Harry Potter! I was on a Wizarding card. Pretty fancy, right?"

Henry couldn't help thinking that Merlin was being kind of braggy, but he was still feeling relieved not to have been kidnapped by an evil madman, so he managed to avoid saying so. Besides, if anyone had a right to be braggy, he supposed Merlin did. He *was* pretty famous.

Merlin continued, "And not just in English. Tales about me have been translated into hundreds of languages. Hundreds! I'm very big in Japan." He set his chin against his chest and grinned at them. One of his teeth wiggled on its own.

"Hey, that reminds me!" said Roy. "Speaking of languages, I was wondering what that first language you spoke was. The language you spoke right before you came out and grabbed Henry."

"Language?" Merlin didn't understand the question. "I only speak one language, but maybe you heard me practicing my backward-speak. It's useful when I want to converse with the Lady of the Lake or anyone who happens to be living inside a mirror."

Emma gasped. "You mean like Alice when she was through the looking glass?"

"Hmph," said Merlin, shaking his head. "Not hardly! That Carroll fellow never could get his facts straight, though he did spin a good yarn. Don't you agree?"

Emma did agree.

"But that means you speak English in Camelot?" asked Roy.

"Goodness, no," said Merlin, laughing. "I don't speak a word of what you call English. I speak a language your world doesn't quite remember, a lovely tongue. Your best professors might call it Devonian, and some might say it was Celt-ish."

"Then how come we can understand you?" asked Roy. "I don't speak Devonian, but I can follow everything you say."

"I'm sure you can," said Merlin. "When you're on a magical adventure, the magic is the language, if you get my drift. Everything that occurs passes through the magic, and it all gets translated. Which gives you instincts you might not otherwise have. On a magic adventure, you'll always understand the lay of the land. You'll be able to choke down foods you couldn't stomach at home, and you'll know the words to songs you've never heard before. That's just the magic at work! Magic transforms you."

"Wait, you aren't speaking English right now?" asked Emma.

"Nope, my pet. In effect, you're speaking Devonian."

"I am?" asked Emma, mightily impressed with herself. She wondered if this was something she could do for show-and-tell in the fall.

"Indeed, and if you leave here and go visit the Temple in Jerusalem, you'll know Aramaic too, or ancient Hebrew, or whatever language might be required of you, depending on the year of your visit. If you go to Venus, you'll be fluent in Venusian."

"Cool!" said Henry.

"That is cool," said Roy, "but then why do characters in books always say old-timey stuff like 'Ods bodkins' and 'By my troth'? If everything gets translated, shouldn't 'Ods bodkins' be translated too, into something like . . .

oh, I don't know . . . 'Gosh!' or maybe 'Dang!'?"

"You——" said Merlin, poking Roy in the chest with a large toad that had hopped up to peer into the bowl of blue flames, "are smarter than you look."

Roy didn't know how to respond to the toad or the compliment, but it didn't matter because Merlin kept on talking. "Downright clever boy. I never even thought about that, but yes, yes, that's so. It *is* silly to have a Frenchman and a Spaniard understanding each other fluently, except when the Frenchman means to say 'Mon Dieu' or the Spaniard cries 'Caramba!' I suppose we should remember that books are often written in the spirit of truth but without proper research, and maybe some books get written by people who never actually stumbled upon magic themselves and so had to imagine it." Merlin began to cough again. "Hargh!"

"That's a nasty cough," said Susan. "Do you have cough syrup in Camelot?"

"Ah, there's no syrup that can help this cough. Comes of gazing into bowls of burning weeds all day," sighed Merlin. "It's an occupational hazard. I should really install better ventilation in this place, but I'm a lazy man, and nobody would understand it anyway. I *do* live in the fifth century."

Henry lifted his eyes from his weed-water dish,

which he had been poking around in. "Is that where we are, the fifth century?"

"No, that's *when* you are, my boy. If I were you, I'd be more precise with my language. *Where* you are is Camelot."

That reminded Henry of something. "But if this really is Camelot, where are King Arthur and all the knights? Asleep?"

Just as Emma had envisioned stained-glass windows and jesters, Henry had imagined swords clashing and jousting tournaments. He wondered if Camelot would be worth a return trip by daylight.

Merlin sighed and ran a hand through his snarled hair. "No, Arthur's off fighting the Saxons, as usual."

"Saxons? What are Saxons?" asked Henry.

"Greedy fellows who like to play with knives and spears, Saxons are. Thieving sorts and mean, drunken louts. Arthur spends all his time battling them. Always with the Saxons. I tell him there's not much point in it, but nobody listens to old Merlin."

"Not much point?"

"No. The Saxons will win in the end, Arthur knows that. And someone else will kill off the Saxons, even-tually. It's just the way things are, but you can't tell Arthur anything. It's in his nature to play with his sword, and honestly, he doesn't listen very well."

Henry, who more than once had the words "poor listening skills" written on his report card, thought for a minute and decided that he would probably rather go off to a glorious battle than sit in a muddy courtyard with a bunch of pigs and burning weeds.

"So, what else is going on, if Arthur's not here?" Henry asked.

"Not much," admitted Merlin. "The pigs root. The chickens lay eggs and peck at each other. The queen wanders around looking stately."

"A queen?" Emma's eyes got big.

"Yes," said Merlin, "and if you want to, you can run along and meet her. Guinevere's generally up about this time of night, rehearsing her despair in the moonlight."

"I want to," said Emma. "I want to see the queen, and this was my wish."

"Fair enough," said the wizard, nodding. "But before you go, a gift!" Merlin motioned to the dishes of weed water, cool in their hands. All this time, Henry, Emma, Susan, and Roy had been holding their dishes carefully. Now they peered into them.

"Just say one word," said Merlin. "One word only. Whisper it into the dish, and the potion will give you a glimpse."

"Just one word?" said Emma. "We shouldn't ask it a question?"

"Heavens, no," said Merlin. "Then you'd only get the future of the first word you asked, which would probably be 'what,' and let me tell you, a glimpse of 'what' is sure to be vague. No fun at all."

"Should we close our eyes?" asked Susan.

Merlin chuckled at the suggestion. "You can, but if you do that, you won't be able to see the glimpse. Visions are awfully visual. Now, who wants to go first? I'm due for a three-day nap as soon as the four of you leave."

"A three-day nap?" Henry couldn't believe that anyone would voluntarily surrender to such a fate.

"Yes, I don't have any visitors scheduled for a bit, and I don't rest easy when I do rest, so I like to put myself to sleep for a good stretch every few weeks. Gives me a chance to dream." Merlin got a faraway look on his face. "Such dreams . . ." He shook his head so that the bird's nest dangled precariously, and pointed at Susan. "You, nearly grown! You go first!"

Susan, startled and unprepared, leaned over her bowl and said the first word that came to mind. She murmured the word "love" and then blushed as soon as she'd said it.

Henry snickered.

Slowly, a wisp of faint smoke curled up from the bowl and turned into what looked like a round picture frame. In the center of the frame was a small group of people jostling each other. Susan couldn't help noticing that at the center of that crowd was a young man in a blue T-shirt, with a shock of blond hair that stood straight up. Only his back was showing, but he had a confident posture and he seemed to be laughing at something. Susan barely noticed the other people standing beside him, until something happened to jerk him so that he almost fell over and toppled onto an old lady.

Henry made a snorting noise in his throat and rolled his eyes, but Susan ignored him and stared at Merlin. "What is it?" she asked. "Who's that guy? Why am I seeing him?"

"I can't answer that for you," said Merlin. "I only know that it's just some part of your future. Fate is limited, my dear, and so are visions. I can show you a moment in your future, but what it will mean to you—well, that's up to you. Free will and all its bothersome trappings." Susan's vision began to fade and the wizard turned his attention to the others. "Now you!" he said, motioning to Henry.

Henry pushed his tongue against his teeth in concentration, thinking deeply before he grinned and said into the bowl, "Trouble."

His wisp rose—a paler color than Susan's—and in

no time at all they were all staring at Henry's picture frame. Inside it was a palm tree on a beach set against a blazing tropical sun. The palm tree waved and small waves rose and fell behind it, crashing to gentle surf before the scene faded.

Henry was indignant. "That's not trouble!" he said. "That's, like, the opposite of trouble!"

"Be careful what you ask for," said Merlin as he watched the scene fade. "You just might get it."

He patted Emma on the head. "Your turn!" he said brightly.

Emma's hands shook as she held her bowl. "Friends?" said Emma, with her lips to the bowl but her eyes on the wizard.

Emma's picture frame rose before her, but inside it was not a person or a scene. It was a plain black oval, a circle of absolute darkness.

"It's broken, I think," she said, shaking her bowl of weed water gently from side to side.

"I don't think so," said Merlin. "My magic is pretty unbreakable. I guess you'll just have to wait and see what that darkness is."

Now it was Roy's turn. "I can't figure out the best word to say," he said. "This magic is tricky."

Merlin laughed. "By definition! Perhaps it's best not

to overthink. That can be just as dangerous as under-thinking, and sometimes far worse. Maybe you should just say the first word that pops into your head."

Roy thought this advice through carefully before he nodded. Then he leaned into his bowl and whispered, "Home!"

His dish steamed and popped and a wisp of smoke curled from it. Inside the frame that hovered in the air, they saw a man. The man looked enormous, as wide as two men and taller than most. He was heavily muscled and angry, squinting into the sun. He opened his mouth in a snarl, but before anyone could tell why, the vision faded.

When Emma saw the man, she shivered. "That was home?" she asked nervously. "He didn't look like home."

"Whoever that man is, he has the posture of a Saxon," muttered Merlin distastefully. Then he slapped his hands together, ready to be done with them. "Well, I guess that's that," he said brightly. "See you around!"

"But, Merlin," Susan said, "that really wasn't home, not at all. We know everyone at home, pretty much, and that man was nobody we know."

Merlin knitted his unruly eyebrows and said, "Per-haps, Susan, there is more to your home than you know.

Places and times and people you've never seen. Things beyond your experience."

Susan said nothing in reply.

"But why would the magic show us that?" asked Emma timidly.

"Oh, little Emma," said Merlin. "Even *I* can't know why magic does what it does, though I know as well as anyone *how* magic does what it does." Then he yawned. "Okay, time's up. I'm off to my nap, but I do hope you've enjoyed your visit. Good night."

"Wait!" said Roy. "What if—"

"No," said Merlin, brushing away Roy's question with a wave of his hands as though it were a flimsy spider web he'd walked through. "No more waiting. We all have visions, and mine wait for me in sleep. You'd best run along."

Saying this, he walked over to the lumpy pile of blankets and leaves, picked his nose and wiped his finger on his sleeve, lay down, and turned over. He waved his hands over his own face and said, "Soporifica!" and before his arms could even drop back down, he began to snore deeply.

The tiny blue fire in the metal bowl blinked out and the room grew cold.

Emma on her own

THERE WAS NO POINT in arguing with the sleeping wizard, and there didn't seem to be any hope of waking him (though Henry poked a few times just to be sure), so the kids crept from the smoky lean-to into the moonlight of the muddy courtyard. When they did, they found that the pigs had run off.

A faint grayness was creeping into the sky above the trees, and this reminded them that although they had not yet seen a knight or a jester, they were going to have to head home. Morning was coming and they had to get to bed before their parents woke up.

"Man, this was kind of a bust," muttered Henry as they started back for the big wooden door. "I thought I might get to joust or slay a dragon or something. Even a small dragon would've been pretty cool."

"The visions were neat," said Susan, blushing again.

"And I liked Merlin, even if he wasn't a princess," said Emma. "He smelled like Halloween."

They all made for the door of the stone castle. Once inside, they started back up the stairs they'd come down, but about halfway up the spiral staircase, they heard a faint sound. Someone was crying.

"The queen!" said Emma excitedly, bouncing up and down. "I want to see the queen. Can we?"

"We don't have time," Susan reminded her.

"Besides," said Henry, "she doesn't sound like much fun at all. Listen."

Emma stuck out her bottom lip. "I don't care," she said. "It's my wish and it's smelly and dark here, and if I don't get to see something pretty, I'll decide to cry." She sat down on the stairs and pouted.

Emma was good most of the time, but when she wanted to, she could be impossible.

"Just what we need," sighed Susan. "Emma in rare form." This was what Mrs. O'Dell called it when Emma misbehaved. "Can't we just let her get the queen's autograph or something?"

Henry shook his head. "I'm not getting in trouble for a dumb queen," he said.

Roy looked at his watch. "I have to side with Henry on this one," he said. "It's time to go."

But Emma refused to budge. She shook her head from side to side. "No!" she said. "No and no and no!" The others were suddenly reminded that she was up waaaay past her bedtime.

Susan sighed, "Look, I'll take her. We'll just go peek in the door, okay, Em? Just one quick minute?" Emma nodded with a pout.

Susan said, "You guys head up without us, and we'll meet you back in the tower room. Cool? That way, if we don't come soon, you can go on ahead and somehow cover for us, and we'll follow right behind."

Roy and Henry agreed (though Roy was nervous about the plan) and turned to head farther up the spiral stairs. Emma and Susan exited the staircase and walked in the direction of the weeping sounds, but they only made it a few feet before they heard a commotion from above: yelling and scrambling and the sound of a ten-year-old being thrown rudely onto a stone step, followed by the sound of another ten-year-old being thrown on top of the first ten-year-old.

Susan and Emma ran back to peer up the dark staircase.

There were more thumping noises and a gruff voice called out, "I don't know who they are, but I know where they're going! Ha-ha-ha!"

A high, squeaky voice said, "We'll see how they like it downstairs."

The girls heard a sharp cry, and the gruff voice said, "Ow! He bit me, this one did. Nasty boy!" After that, Henry yelled and Roy yelled and then everyone was yelling.

It sounded to Susan and Emma as though the boys put up a valiant effort, but somewhere on the staircase, the men got the upper hand, and Henry and Roy were subdued. The girls ducked out of sight as everyone stomped down the stairs past them. They caught only a quick glimpse of two leather-clad men carrying their large spears and Henry and Roy.

As he was carried past, Henry made sure to yell at the top of his lungs, "Ods bodkins! I wish there was someone to help us. I wish we weren't all alone in this castle, just the two of us by our lonesome selves. That way we'd have someone to break us out of the dungeon!"

When Susan and Emma were sure they were alone again, Susan said, "Wait here. I'm just going to see how far down the staircase goes, but I can move faster on my own. Just don't let anyone see you, okay?"

Emma's lip began to tremble. "I'm sorry I made a bad wish," she said. "I'm sorry I wanted to see the queen."

Susan leaned over and hugged Emma. "It isn't your

fault, Em," she said. "Not at all, but we need to rescue Roy and Henry right now! Look!" She pointed down the hallway behind Emma to a small shuttered window. The sky beyond the window was growing light. "It's getting to be morning," she said, "and once it's morning here, it's morning at home too. I think."

"Oh," said Emma. "Oh!"

"Yeah, and we are going to be in big, big trouble if we aren't all back in the tower soon, so can you just stay put?"

Emma nodded, trying not to cry, as Susan stepped into the staircase and headed down the stairs. But then—more terrible luck! Just as Susan disappeared into the dark spiral of stairs, Emma heard the sound of more heavy feet from above, and another voice, this one firm and official, called down, "I think that's the last of 'em. No more scamps to be seen!"

As the feet and the firm voice marched past the doorway where Emma stood, she held her breath, waiting, waiting, waiting to see what would happen, and then—

Susan squealed below, and Emma heard her shrieking, "Hands off me, you loser! You big dumb freak!" There was a thunking sound that Emma thought might have been Susan kicking the stone walls of the staircase, and a series of grunts that didn't sound at all like Susan.

Emma stuck her head in the hallway. She could make out the sound of one good hard slap and an "oof!" but then the firm voice said "Got 'er!" and the noise in the stairwell ceased.

Emma was all alone and she didn't have the slightest idea what to do. The hallway was silent except for the faint noise of the queen crying. Emma wished there were someone to ask for advice. She wished she had time to think for a while, but there wasn't any time—not if they wanted to get home before their parents woke up, which they most certainly did.

How had this happened? Emma was never on her own, except when she was sleeping or in the bathroom (neither of which counted). She couldn't remember being left alone for more than a minute in her life, not ever. She was lonely sometimes, sure, but there was always someone nearby, keeping an eye out. Someone was always telling her what to do. Her mother even laid her clothes on a chair every night before she went to bed. She'd wished a hundred times to be left in charge of herself, but it had never actually happened. Now, here she was with no practice at being alone and with what seemed like an awfully big job to do.

But she wasn't getting anywhere sitting on the floor

of the hallway, so she got up. She figured that if she didn't want to do this all alone, she needed to ask for help, and since Merlin was fast asleep, she decided to find the queen. She followed the sound of weeping down the hallway and to another wooden door, which stood cracked open just the slightest bit. She peeked around the door, and gasped.

Why?

Because Guinevere was all that Emma had hoped for in a queen. At last, here was Camelot as Emma had imagined it. For just a moment, she forgot about Henry, Roy, and Susan as she gazed at the splendor before her. The queen stood directly across the room from Emma. Even from behind, Emma could tell that Guinevere was beautiful—tall and willowy, clothed in a heavy green gown, with long black hair that tumbled down her narrow back, hair that could only be described as tresses. Silver thread was laced in and out of her tresses, and flowers were tossed casually about her feet. On the wall before the queen was a mirror of polished metal, and Guinevere gazed into it. Emma stared, awestruck, at the gorgeous reflection.

Although she continued to make weeping sounds, the queen didn't look like she was crying. Her shoulders didn't shake and there were no actual tears on her face.

It was as though she was practicing for a play. She stared at herself as she wept. She stared into the mirror and looked almost pleased.

Emma remembered Henry, Roy, and Susan, but she couldn't help staring for a minute longer at Guinevere's reflection in the mirror. Guinevere was *that* perfect. When the queen stopped making the crying sounds and took something from a tiny box in her hand, Emma craned her neck to see what it was. Without meaning to, she pushed on the door, which gave way with a cree-ea-ea-kkk. Emma froze, and the queen turned gracefully, slowly, and stared.

Neither of them spoke for a heartbeat, but then Emma saw what the queen held: a butterfly. In one hand, she held the body of the butterfly, and in the other, a single wing. The queen tilted her head to one side and thoughtfully rubbed the wing along her face, leaving a trail of shimmering lavender along her finely arched cheekbone. "Hello," she said. She leaned forward and reached out a hand. "Are you a girl? Can it really be that there's a girl in my castle? Oh. For joy." Although the queen smiled and reached out to Emma, her voice sounded as passionless as her weeping had looked.

Something inside Emma said "Run!" Something told

her that a flat-voiced queen who breaks butterflies and cries without tears is not the kind of queen who helps little girls rescue their brother and friends. Emma. turned and fled to the stairwell, and when she got there, since down meant the dungeon, Emma ran up.

Behind her, the queen called out in a voice that fell on Emma like snow, soft but cold, "Hello? Little girl? Oh, please come and visit with me. It's so lonely in the castle. I have nobody to play with at all."

When Emma, skittering up the stone stairs, heard the queen behind her, she stopped and almost turned. Despite her eerily even tones, the queen did sound lonely. But the sound of Guinevere's heels clicking purposefully along on the stone floor frightened Emma, so she ran even faster, her heart pounding. She took the stairs two at a time, which was no easy feat, since the stairs were as steep as Emma's legs were short.

Behind her, she could hear the queen moving faster too, though still in long, even strides. As she grew closer to Emma, Guinevere's voice changed and became a little harder. "Little girl, why won't you listen to me? Why does nobody listen to me? Little girl, just what are you doing in my castle?"

When Emma didn't answer, the voice turned sharp. "I thought we could be friends," called the queen. "I thought you'd come to visit me, but you're leaving, like Arthur, like everyone." Then the footsteps ceased and the queen clapped her hands and called loudly so that her steely voice rang in the stairwell. "Guards!" she cried. "To the tower! We have an intruder! A little sneak!"

Immediately, footsteps began to tromp up the stone steps from below.

If the queen had been a little more hot-blooded and willing to run, she'd probably have caught Emma herself, but she stopped on the stair instead, trusting that her guards were on their way, so Emma arrived in the top tower room alone.

She looked at the wall and thought of home. She looked at the stairs and thought of the dungeon. She looked at the lightening sky through the window and thought of her parents. What to do? She asked herself what Susan would do, but no answer came.

The thunder of feet was on the stairs. The day was coming, and so were the guards. Emma sat down on the cold stone floor, lost. She was tired and confused. For a second, she closed her eyes and wondered if maybe this was all a dream. She thought perhaps if she fell asleep, she'd wake up at home in her comfy bed, but this thought made her feel like a baby and she hated that feeling, so she opened her eyes and gritted her teeth. She waited for the guards to come and take her to the dungeon with the others, where she knew she'd be locked forever in a pit of snakes or bugs and fed only bread and water.

Suddenly a thought struck her—a good thought! Afterward, she couldn't explain how she knew—just knew—that the wall would help her. It only made sense. It was a wishing wall, after all, and this was her wish.

As the guards filed into the room, Emma stood up. She stared the leather-clad brutes in the eyes and placed her palm flat against the wall. Quickly, but without any fear of their spears, she said in a whisper so that the men only heard a sssssssss sound, "Home, Mister Wall? Please?"

Then Emma was in the cornfield, and dawn was breaking rosy, leaking into the sky. Without missing a beat, she wished again, "Now can we go back? To the dungeon this time? To Susan? And Henry and Roy?"

The wall obeyed, and there she was, in the dungeon!

Emma stood at the very bottom of the deep spiral of stone, in the first cell in a long chain of cells, but she couldn't see the stairs or the cell because there was no light. Not a single speck.

Have you ever been in absolute darkness?

Really?

I don't believe you, because it doesn't happen often. Even deep in the back of your closet, there is a sliver of light under the door. Even at midnight, there are a few stars. This was total, complete darkness. It looked like a piece of black paper. It looked like—Emma's vision! In fact, it was Emma's vision.

"But that's no fun!" said Emma to herself when she realized this.

As her voice echoed, she heard Susan say in a startled, scared voice, "Who's there?"

Emma, now glad that the dungeon guards had all followed her to the tower, said, "It's me, me Emma. Don't worry, I'm here!" It felt good to say that. Emma felt like an ambulance, like a superhero, flying to the rescue.

She heard Susan's disbelieving voice. "Emma?"

"Yep," she said as casually as she could. "Yep, it's me."

"Emma?" Susan's voice jumped in the dark. "How'd you get here?"

"I don't have time to explain," said Emma. "Give me your hand."

As Susan's hand flailed in the darkness and finally found her own, it occurred to Emma that she'd never had anything to explain before or anyone to explain things to. She was always asking questions. It felt good having the answer, for once. She beamed in the darkness, and with one hand on the wall and the other holding Susan's fingers tightly, she stretched out Susan's arm so that Susan cried, "Yow, Em! What're you doing?"

But Emma, ignoring Susan's cries, just brushed her friend's fingers roughly against the wall and said, "Please, Mister Wall, take us home?"

The wall did exactly as she asked. Emma and Susan blinked quickly into the field and then out again at Emma's soft request to be with Henry and Roy. Before Susan even figured out what was happening, they were deep within the dark maze of cells where the boys were being held captive.

Emma chirped, "Hey, Hen. Hey, Roy!"

"What? Huh?" said Henry. "How'd you get here?"

Again, with no explanation, Emma grabbed at her brother and Roy. She pulled them to her and pushed them against her wall. Joyfully, proudly, she turned to make her wish.

Except that this time, Susan beat her to it, and although Emma never quite forgave Susan for stealing her moment, it should be explained that Susan wasn't really trying to be bossy. She just was an older sister doing what older sisters do. She almost couldn't help it when she whispered into the darkness, "Wall, I think we're ready to go home."

Then they were back in the cornfield beyond Quiet Falls, home for good, or at least for the night (or rather the morning).

And then they were turning the key in the wall to lock it.

And then they were gathering their bikes, wet with dew, and riding home through the early light of an Iowa dawn.

And then Emma and Henry were at their home, safe in their beds, just in time for their dad to shout out, "Up and at 'em! Who wants the first shower?"

But Susan and Roy were not quite so lucky. They arrived in their kitchen and were still panting from the ride when their mother wandered in wearing a bright red bathrobe. They froze, and Susan said, "Hey, Mom, we were just—"

But they didn't need to worry because (thank goodness) most grown-ups are no good in the morning.

"I do *not* want to know," Mrs. Levy murmured, holding up a hand. "I have a long day ahead of me, and I just want my coffee." She reached for a mug, groaned, and mumbled something about summer vacation being anything but.

The Worst Pirate in the World

HOW EMMA AND HENRY managed to stagger through breakfast without their parents noticing their utter exhaustion is anyone's guess, but they did so with droopy eyes. As soon as their parents left for work, each of them fell fast asleep, and it wasn't until well after lunchtime that Roy and Susan (who'd had a similar morning) thumped up the porch steps to rouse their friends.

At the sound of the doorbell, Emma and Henry rolled out of their beds. They splashed water on their faces, brushed the fuzzy sweaters from their teeth, pulled on their clothes, and wolfed down a quick lunch of potato chips and chocolate milk, which would have horrified their parents but tasted just right. Then they headed out into the hot afternoon, vague and cloudy-headed.

It's always strange, waking late in the day, but when you have just returned from a magical adventure to fifth-century England, where you have spent several hours visiting with a world-famous wizard, well, when that is the case, waking late in the day is really disorienting. Especially when you still have magical visions to figure out and rules you don't understand.

Once they were outside sitting on the porch steps, and the afternoon sun had helped to burn off some of their confusion as though it were the morning haze on a field, Roy turned to Susan.

"Wow," he said. "That was pretty amazing, what you guys did last night, rescuing us from the dungeon like that. How did you know you didn't need the key to go back and forth with the wall?"

"I didn't," said Susan with a note of apology in her voice. "It was all Emma. I got caught too, walked right into the guards after they grabbed you guys. Emma rescued me right before she came for you."

"Really?" Roy looked impressed. "I just assumed you were the commander of the mission, but wow, Emma!" He turned his attention to the younger girl. "Good job! How'd you figure it out?"

Emma rubbed her eyes, which were still itchy with sleep, and answered slowly. "I—I didn't figure anything out. I didn't even think of the key until now. I just—just wished. The queen was coming after me and I got scared and it just felt like it would work."

"Well, however you did it," Roy continued, "we all owe you a big thank-you."

Emma turned red, which looked funny against her white-blond hair. "Sure thing," said Emma. "I mean, you too. I mean, you're welcome."

"Yeah, no kidding," chimed in Henry. "I don't think I could have handled it by myself. We'd probably still be stuck in Camelot if it was up to me." He bumped Emma, who was sitting on the step beside him, with his elbow. "Good job, Em!"

Emma beamed at her brother.

"It's important that we know we can do that, blink back and forth without having to use the key," said Roy, "but it makes me a little confused. Why do we need the key sometimes, but not others?"

"You're overthinking again," Henry said wearily. "Obviously, we need the key at the beginning of each adventure to kind of rev up the wall, but then once it's running, it just keeps on."

"How do you know that for sure?" asked Roy. "When is the adventure officially over?"

Henry didn't answer, which meant that he didn't

know, though it might also have meant that he considered "officially" to be in the same category as "technically." That is to say, in the category of "Things Roy should stop worrying so much about."

"Hey, guys?" Emma stood up and turned around to face the others on the steps. "I've been thinking about something."

"What's that?" asked Susan.

"Well, when I first showed up in the dungeon, it was really dark," said Emma.

"Yeah," said Henry. "We know, we were there too, but don't worry, there's nothing to be scared about now. We're home safe."

Emma furrowed her brow and said, "No, you don't understand. I'm not saying I was scared. I'm saying that it was dark, that it looked like my vision, dark like the color black. I think it was my vision. My glimpse."

"Ah," said Henry. "I get it now!"

"That's interesting," said Roy, "and it makes sense because Emma's word was 'friends,' and we were all there in the darkness. Maybe each of our visions is a glimpse of something that will happen when we use the magic. That'd be neat. We'd kind of know what to look for."

"But," said Susan, thinking back to her own vision,

"nobody else has run into their vision, have they?"

"That makes sense too," said Roy, "because Camelot was Emma's wish."

Everybody pondered this.

"I don't understand, though," said Emma. "Does this mean that no matter what we wish for, no matter where we go, we'll see the same thing? I don't understand."

"I doubt it," said Roy. "I mean, it doesn't seem likely that the big ugly guy from my glimpse is capable of just popping up anywhere. Maybe we're just kind of fated to choose the wishes we'll choose."

"No way!" said Henry. "That can't be true. I haven't even decided what my wish is yet. I know I've been saying I'd pick pirates, but what if I don't? I could always change my mind at the last second. How could the wall know, or Merlin know, or a bunch of steaming weeds know what I'm going to wish for? I'm not stuck! I refuse to be stuck. I'll change my mind. I'll change it twice! How could I possibly be stuck?" He looked at Roy.

But even Roy had no answer for this. None of them did. After all, wise old philosophers have been struggling with the idea of fate for thousands of years, and it's unlikely (although not entirely impossible) that four kids would be able to work it out in a matter of minutes.

Susan tried, though, saying simply, "Maybe it doesn't

exactly make sense. Maybe that's why it's magic. I wouldn't worry about it too much, though, because Merlin only said that some of what we'd bump into was fated. He didn't say what we'd do was fated. Right?"

"Let's hope so, for your sake!" hooted Henry, who felt a little better on hearing this. "I can't wait to see what you decide to do with that blond boy you're going to bump into. You going to ask him on a date?" Henry made a romantic kissy face, or what he imagined to be a romantic kissy face, though he actually looked more like a nearsighted goldfish.

Susan decided to change the subject. "However it works," she said, "can we please get started already? We have a lot to do today, and we're getting a late start."

So they hopped on their bikes and got moving, and kept moving. In about twenty minutes, they were at the wall, and Henry was brandishing the key with a grin.

"My turn!" he said. "Arrr, mateys?"

"How," asked Susan, "do you plan to accomplish this, being that pirates hang out on ships all the time?"

"Yeah," said Henry, "but ships have walls too."

"I don't think so," said Susan. "They aren't build-ings, at least not the way everything else has been so far. Why don't you wish for something else? Let's go to China—there's a great big wall there!"

Henry rolled his eyes. "Could you possibly be any more boring? Why don't we just stay home and watch public television."

"Okay, then what about American history?" asked Roy, who liked public television. "We could meet George Washington!"

Henry fell heavily to the ground, groaning. "Ugh," he said, "I am dying of boredom at the mere thought! Gah, the boring genes must run in your family."

Emma piped up, "Pirates must go somewhere when their ships are getting fixed. We could visit a pirate at home, when he's on break."

Henry looked up from his spot on the ground. "Hey, that's not a bad idea," he said. "You're right. Just because pirates spend most of their time on the high seas doesn't mean they don't sometimes set foot in buildings. They must have someplace they go when they're on land, a pirate hotel or something. We just need to wish to be in a building with a pirate." He stood up and brushed the dirt from his pants. "Everyone get into position. No time to waste!"

Everyone lined up at the wall and held a hand out to the rough stone. Henry turned the key and wished.

"I wish we were in a pirate house," he said, "where we could meet a pirate—a really bad pirate, the worst pirate in the world!" He added an extra "Arrr!" to set the tone.

In the blink of an eye, the scenery shifted, and they were all standing on plank floors, surrounded by old-looking furniture. Through the one front window in the room, they could see gray-blue water and sea grasses waving gently on sandy dunes. In another room, they could hear someone rustling about. On the wall across from them were all manner of interesting trinkets hung in an old fishing net, and on either side of the net, tall bookshelves were filled to bursting.

Emma kept her hand on the wall nervously, just in case they should need to make a speedy getaway, but after a minute, when nothing terrible had happened, she let it fall to her side.

After looking around, Henry called out, "Hello? Is there a pirate here?"

Whoever was rustling in the next room dropped something heavy and called out in a deep, quiet voice, "Who's there?"

A man came and stood in the door between the two rooms. "Yes, hello?" said the man. "Can I help you?"

The man did not look like a pirate in the least. He was clean-shaven and neat as a pin, as well washed as Merlin had been filthy. He wore old-fashioned breeches that buckled at the knee and a billowy white shirt—a clean one. There wasn't a rat or a spot of bird poop in sight. His pants were old but nicely mended, and he had a book in one hand. He stared at them.

The stare was awkward. Finally Henry said, "We, um. We were hoping to see a pirate. We thought we were coming to a pirate house. Are there any around?"

The man cleared his throat and smiled. He set his book on a little table and said proudly, "As a matter of fact, you did come to a pirate house. Perhaps the most famous pirate house in the history of pirate houses. Many a ferocious fellow has trod these planks. They were ripped mercilessly from a number of unfortunate ships."

"Really?" asked Henry, staring down at the planks.

"Indeed, though I'm afraid I'm not a very good example of a pirate, myself. Truly, I'm the worst pirate in the world." It was clear from the way he said this that he didn't mean what Henry had meant when he'd uttered the same phrase. The man sighed, "I suppose by the standards of some bloodthirsty seamen, I'm hardly a pirate at all."

The kids all stared at him blankly.

"But," said Roy, "you said this was the home of a famous pirate."

"Oh, it was," said the man, looking back up and nodding emphatically.

"And it's also your house," continued Roy. "So that would suggest—"

The man cut Roy off with a nod. "It's mine now, but these walls have known better buccaneers than yours truly. It was my father's before me."

"Your father?" asked Susan.

"Yes, my papa, Blackbeard, the scourge of the seas. This was his house."

"Blackbeard lived on land?" Henry sounded skeptical.

"Not for long, but for a few years. He ran his ship aground one day, not far from here, just down the Carolina coast. While he was on shore buying rum, he met my mom."

"Your mom?" asked Susan. "I've never heard of Mrs. Blackbeard."

"Thank goodness she didn't hear you say that!" the man laughed. "How she hated it when people called Papa Blackbeard. Her married name was Mrs. Edward Teach, but her friends called her Charlotte." The man spoke these words with a fond and slightly wistful look in his eye. "She was a lovely woman. She was shy but oh, could she dance. And sometimes she let me win at cards!"

"Why are you such a bad pirate?" asked Emma. "I think you seem nice."

"That's just it," said the man with a despairing look. "I *am* nice. I haven't been able to live up to my father's legend, not at all. My name is Sam," he said, sticking out a hand for shaking. "But it was supposed to be"— he choked on the next word—"Junior."

Emma shook his hand. She felt very sorry for Sam.

Henry, who didn't want the pirate part of the story derailed, prodded. "You were saying your dad lived here—"

"Yes, he tried to settle down and lead a different kind of life. He fixed up the place, painted the roof, and worked in the garden when he wasn't drinking, but life on land didn't agree with him at all. He kept getting drunk and shooting holes in the roof, and then it would rain and we'd all get wet. Eventually he went back to his ship and left us behind, here, in this house." Sam looked like he might cry.

"I'm sorry," said Susan.

"That's so nice of you to say," Sam said, brightening. "It wasn't all bad. He did stop in to visit from time to time and bring me presents." He gestured to the wall hung with the net. Tucked up in it were shrunken heads, monkey paws, strands of black pearls, and dried seaweed. "He always remembered my birthday," Sam added fondly.

"What happened after that?" asked Roy curiously.

"Eventually some farmers got fed up with his raiding and marauding and cut off his head. And thank goodness too. Though he was my father, and I loved him, he was a mean, mean man, birthday presents aside. He used to set lit matches into the brim of his hat and make scary faces when he was supposed to be reading me bedtime stories."

Emma gave a shiver at the thought.

"It sounds exciting to me!" said Henry.

"Parents aren't supposed to be exciting," said Sam. "Parents are supposed to love you unconditionally, feed you, and occasionally bounce you on their knee, though that doesn't work so well when your father has a peg leg. Parents are supposed to be trustworthy, dependable—"

"You mean boring?" asked Henry.

"I'd take boring over marauding, any day," said Sam.

Emma nodded in sympathy. "Gosh, that does sound hard," she said.

"It was," said Sam. "I had nightmares all the time. After he was gone, my mother married a shopkeeper and we all settled down inland, which was fine, but when my mother passed away, I came back here to live. I like the sound of the waves."

Roy remembered something. "But wait—you did say you're a pirate too. Didn't you?"

"Sure, I'm a pirate, officially," said Sam. "I have a certificate of authenticity." He pointed to a framed piece of parchment on the wall, written in blood and with a great blob of red wax at the bottom. "I had a buccaneer's baptism and everything, but I didn't have much choice in the matter. There's a lot of pressure, when you're a second-generation pirate, to carry on the family name, but I—I couldn't—" Sam began to clear his throat. He didn't finish his sentence.

"Couldn't what?" asked Emma, looking at the shrunken heads and imagining the terrible things Sam had not been able to do.

"I couldn't grow a beard." Sam put a hand over his eyes. "It was terrible. Every time my father came home from the seas, he'd take me out in the yard and examine my face in the sunlight, looking for the least little shimmering blond hairs, but it was no use. Finally he gave up and left me alone, a disgrace to his name."

"That does sound awful," said Susan.

"There are perks, though," said Sam. "I own a pirate ship, my inheritance—"

"Cool!" said Henry.

Sam continued wistfully, "But it's off in Ile Perdida, and I've never been able to get down there to see it. I'm too busy here."

"You are?" said Roy. "With what?"

"I'm putting together an archive," said Sam proudly, pointing to the shelves, "full of leaflets and pictures and books about pirates. I aim to have the best pirate archive in the world. It's my little way of following in his footsteps, I suppose." He added a weak, "Arr?"

Roy looked interested. "Do you want to be an archivist," he asked, "or a pirate?"

"Well, I'd like to think I'm sort of both," said Sam. "Keeping the dream alive on paper. I mean, I do love my books, and a pirate's life is kind of hard and wet, and there's always the risk of being forced to walk the plank," he said thoughtfully. "But it sounds like a lot of fun too, what with all the boats and booty—and I wouldn't have to be nearly so evil as my papa," Sam sighed. "It doesn't matter, though, since I can't be a pirate without a beard. It just isn't proper."

"That," said Henry, "is just about the stupidest thing I've ever heard in my life. You don't have to call yourself Blackbeard Junior. You can be your own kind of pirate. No-Beard the Pirate. Or Bald-Chin the Pirate. Or Sam the Pirate, if you don't feel especially creative! But you've got the ship, so why not?"

Sam looked put out. "It's not that easy," he said. "You make it all sound so simple. Papa's ship—the *Queen Anne's Revenge*—is far away on an island. How am I going to get there without a ship? You see my problem?"

"I think," said Susan kindly, "that sounds a little like an excuse. Are you maybe just afraid?"

Sam protested, "Who, me, afraid? Bah! It's complicated. I mean, really, I haven't ever even seen the ship. It could be in terrible shape or stolen by now. What if I went all the way to Ile Perdida to get the thing, and it wasn't there?"

"That's not a very good excuse," said Roy. "You'd be having an adventure, and you'd get to chase down the people who stole the ship. Obviously!"

The others nodded in agreement. "I think your father would be ashamed," Henry said. "I mean, if he couldn't grow a beard, don't you think he'd just find a way to make that seem like a good thing? He'd have said that beards got in the way of real piracy. Or that he'd had his beard torn off in a brawl or something. Why, he'd probably have set a trend, and all the pirates would have started shaving, just to be like him!"

Sam considered this. "My father *was* pretty popular," he said, "for a dastardly villain."

"I think," said Henry, "that you are just a big chicken."

Sam's face fell, but Henry proceeded to make buck-buck-buck sounds.

This was too much for Sam to take. After all, the blood of Blackbeard did run in his veins, however weakly.

"I'm not a chicken!" he sputtered at Henry. "Why, if I had a way to get to Ile Perdida, I'd go right now! This very minute!"

Henry stopped teasing and looked Sam up and down. "Really?"

"Yes, really," said Sam.

"Then maybe we can help you," said Henry. He put his hand flat against the wall.

When they saw this, the others stepped over to the wall and did the same.

"Are you sure about this, Henry?" asked Roy. "It seems a little wrong."

"Sure about what?" asked Sam.

"He said he wanted to," said Henry.

"Wanted to what?" asked Sam.

When he noticed their movements, he backed up a

few feet. "Wait! What kind of fiendish children are you? How did you get in here, anyway? Hold on a second!"

"Come on," said Henry, patting the wall. "If you don't like it, we promise to bring you back here. Or are you chicken?"

"Um, n-n-no—" Sam began to stammer. "But if we're really going, I need to wash some socks for the trip, and I'll have to pack a bag, and really I don't know what the weather is like there. Pretty humid, I think, not good at all for my asthma—"

"Never mind all that!" Henry grabbed Sam's hand and pulled him to the wall (which was only a matter of a few feet in the very small cottage).

Sam, stumbling forward, said, "At least let me feed the cat—"

But he wasn't fast enough. Henry muttered something, and in the blink of an eye, they were all staring at the familiar green field.

Only it wasn't at all familiar to Sam. "Where am I?" asked Sam. "How did you do that? What kind of twitchy magic do you children have?"

Henry ignored him and began to wish again.

But Susan said, "Wait a second, Henry. We need to talk. I don't know how I feel about kidnapping this guy. We should explain the wall."

"Yes," said Sam, "you should explain!"

"Look, we can always take him home if he wants to go back," said Henry, "but we can't tell him about it. We swore."

"We can take him with us through the wall, but we can't tell him about it? That's silly." Susan shook her head.

"I'm with Susan," said Roy. "I think we need to explain. That way he won't be so scared. Right?" he asked Sam.

Sam nodded. He wasn't exactly sure what he was agreeing to, but he was all for being less scared.

After they briefly explained about the wall, Sam's eyes glittered with a tiny shine. "Okay," he said, "I'm in. We'll head for Ile Perdida and we'll take a look at the *Queen Anne's Revenge,* see what kind of shape she's in, but I'm not promising anything yet. After all, she could be very dirty." Sam made a fastidious face.

They all touched the wall, and Henry said, "Blackbeard's house on Ile Perdida," but nothing happened, so he tried again. "Whatever building is standing nearest the *Queen Anne's Revenge.*"

Lickety-split, the wall under their hands turned to thatched palm fronds, and they were staring at birds. Birds everywhere. Around them, the air was extremely hot, like an open oven door.

"I'm surprised this even counts as a wall," said Susan, inspecting the straw mat beneath her hand. It was really more like a bus stop made of palm fronds than it was like a building. There was a thatched roof overhead, but that was about it. Susan stepped out onto the sand to look around and Emma ran ahead of her to hunt for shells.

Sam wiped his forehead right away. "Goodness, I feel faint," he said.

"But look!" cried Roy, pointing. Off a ways, in the distance, a ship was bobbing on the waves.

Sam did not look refreshed by the sight of his ship.

"Let's go check it out!" called Henry, tugging on Sam's sleeve. "It's your inheritance, your father's legacy. Let's go!"

"No, no, no—this will never do," said Sam fussily, looking around. "Where will I keep all my books?"

"You don't have to live here," said Henry. "You can go anywhere you want once you get the ship in shape."

"I guess," said Sam, sounding a little whiny, especially for a fully grown man who has just laid eyes on his pirate ship. He took a minute to breathe in the air and look around. "But it's awful hot in the meantime." He fanned himself.

Roy had stepped out from the shade of the hut and

was peering down the beach at the pirate ship (and at Susan and Emma, who were taking off their shoes) when Sam's whiny tone shifted ever so slightly.

"No," Sam said, "I don't think I like it here. I don't think I like it at all. The southern seas don't suit me, but you know, there are many ways to buccaneer, and this"—he patted the straw wall beside him—"gives me an idea."

Only Henry heard this, and only Henry noticed when Sam laid a hand on the palm fronds deliberately. Emma and Susan were already wading into the shallows and Roy was studying a sea turtle when Sam uttered the words, "I wish I was—"

"No!" shouted Henry, hurling himself toward Sam.

And though he had no time to stop the pirate, he did manage to touch the wall of the hut before Sam could say, "back at that wall."

Many Ways to Buccaneer

EMMA AND SUSAN, watching from the beach, yelled and then ran barefoot in the direction of the thatched hut. Roy heard their cries and turned to see what all the fuss was about. All three of them dashed over to the wall and wished breathlessly to be home, but nothing happened!

"We're stranded," cried Susan. "We're stuck!"

"We are?" asked Emma. "What will we do?" Her chin quivered.

"Not much *to* do," said Roy, patting her shoulder. "We just have to wait, but I'm sure it'll turn out fine." He looked at Susan for confirmation of this fact. "Henry will come right back for us. Won't he?"

"Of course he will," said Susan. Under her breath she added, "If he can."

But Emma didn't hear that part, so she breathed a

sigh of relief. "Can we go swimming?" she asked.

Susan was about to say no because she thought they should wait by the wall for Henry, but when she looked out at the greenish blue water, she changed her mind. It did look tantalizing. "Okay," she said, "I guess our clothes will dry fast in this sun, but we have to be extra careful and stay close to shore. Who knows how many miles we are from the nearest lifeguard."

Roy took off his sneakers and they all walked into the water, which felt as good as it looked. They paddled and watched tiny fish dart around their feet, and it was nothing like the murky brown reservoir they swam in at home. None of them had ever gone swimming in their clothes before, and they laughed when their shirts filled with big air bubbles. But when a dark shark fin broke the surface of the sea only about twenty feet away, they all climbed quickly back onto the sand, licking the salt from their lips.

Meanwhile, Henry and Sam arrived in the cornfield side by side. They eyed each other up and down, with their hands still firmly plastered to the wall.

Henry wasn't someone who believed in thinking too hard about things, so he moved quickly. As soon as he saw that they were back home, he grabbed Sam, toppled them both to the ground, and held the man down for about twelve seconds. Unfortunately, Sam was more than twice his size and rolled Henry off in no time, pushed himself back to standing, and dusted off his britches.

Henry frowned. He only knew one way to over-power a grown-up, and that was by tickling, a technique he often practiced on his dad. He'd never imagined the skill would come in handy in an actual fight, but he was ready to try anything. He jumped to his feet and gave a battle cry. With his hands outstretched and his fingers flexed, he charged and tickled the would-be pirate mercilessly so that Sam fell back onto the ground.

"No, no, hee heee heee, ho, help!" cried Sam. "It's just what all the sea dogs used to do. Oh, help, help, he-eh-eh-elp. Please, please stop!" he called out breath-lessly, laughing hysterically in that not-really-happy way that accompanies a serious tickling session.

"Promise you won't jump up?" shouted Henry as he tickled. "Promise you'll stay put? Promise—on the pirate's code!"

"I promise, I promise, I promise!" panted Sam.

Henry stopped tickling, but as soon as he stopped, Sam lunged at the wall again. Henry dove after him and barely had time to touch the wall before Sam called out in a rush, "I wish I was in a bank full of gold!"

Suddenly they were in a small room, surrounded by stacks and stacks of money. Neither Henry nor Sam was willing to take his hand from the wall, but Sam reached down and groped in a bag at his feet. When he drew out his hand, his fingers were wrapped tightly around a bundle of old-fashioned-looking money. He cackled, "Now, this is fun! I could loot all day! At last I understand why my mean old papa ran back to the sea and the ships and the suckers!"

Henry eyed Sam angrily without taking his hand from the wall. "You promised," he said, "on the pirate's code."

Sam shrugged, sniffing his handful of bills. "You can't hold me to that. There *is* no such thing as the pirate's code."

"Oh," said Henry. "I thought there was."

"Nope, and if there were a pirate's code, it would probably be 'Do what you want, and never mind about the mess.' Plus, you were tickling me, and that's downright unfair. You can't expect someone to keep a promise they make when they're being tickled."

"That might be," said Henry, "but you deserved it for stealing the wall from us. Why did you do that?"

"I was being a pirate," Sam said matter-of-factly.

"What do you think pirates do? They steal stuff from people, and you're people."

"But that's crummy," said Henry, who had never considered what it might feel like to be pirated from. "That's not adventurous or exciting or glorious. That's just being a bully."

"Well, sure!" said Sam with a laugh. "And just imagine what a bully I could be! With that wall, I could be the ultimate pirate without ever getting seasick. I could steal from everyone, work from home, and never even get sunburned. A whole new breed of pirate! My papa would be so proud."

Henry thought this was actually kind of clever, but it didn't really change anything. "You could have stranded us there forever," he said. "With no food or water. You *have* stranded Roy and Susan and Emma! Do you want to be a pirate badly enough to leave a bunch of kids to starve? On a desert island? In the past?"

"It wasn't a desert island," said Sam, neatly counting his stack of bills, "and I'd have come back for you. I just wanted a little booty and some respect."

"Respect from who?" asked Henry.

"Why, my father's old sea dog friends. They stop in periodically to dig holes in the yard to see if they can find Blackbeard's treasure. They eat my food and laugh at my books and get their big swashbuckling boots all over my good rugs. Ha! I'd show them!"

Henry could understand this desire and felt for Sam, but all the same, this behavior was out of line. "Too bad it isn't your wall," he said. He turned to the vault wall and added, "Home, please."

In a blink, they were back in the field in the shadow of the wall.

Sam eyed Henry up and down. "You're no fun, and anyway, who says it's *your* wall?" Then he turned to the wall and said, "The bank!"

They were back in the bank in a flash, and Sam's greedy fingers were scrabbling around in another bag.

"It's our wall because we found it first!" said Henry, and then to the wall he said again, "Home!"

Instantly, they were back in the field, only now, Sam had two bundles of bills.

"In that case," said Sam, "I found it too—right after you did. You aren't the first people in the world to find it, you know!" He stuffed the money in his shirt and turned back to the wall. "The bank!" he said.

They were back in the bank, and Sam was rooting in a bag of coins on the shelf beside him.

Henry sighed. In a tired voice he said, "Home, please!"

They were back in the field just as before, only this time, Sam had been holding onto the burlap sack the money was in, so he had the entire bag with him! With the weight of all the money, the bag was incredibly heavy and it fell sharply to the ground, spilling gold and silver coins all over the grass. Sam laughed in delight. "Look at all that!"

Henry was feeling funny from all of the switcheroo-ing. "Please stop?" he begged. "Please? We aren't getting anywhere, and this could go on all day."

"Speak for yourself," said Sam. "I'm getting some-where. I'm getting rich." He kicked at the pile of coins but did not take his hand from the wall. "Okay," he said to the wall with a greedy grin, "now I want to be in the biggest bank in the history of the world!"

Instantly, they were in the biggest bank in the his-tory of the world. Only it wasn't quite what Sam had bargained for. He meant to arrive in the biggest bank in the history of the world as he knew it, but the history of the world is long and extends in both directions. Suddenly Sam found himself in a very strange place: a highly secure, high-tech, ultramodern bank vault!

Under their hands, a metal wall looked to Henry like it was made of some kind of futuristic metal. It felt solid but looked like mercury, like a silvery flowing river. Laser beams crisscrossed the walls in roving strands of multicolored light. The walls were not simple shelves full of bags of coins, bars of gold, and stacks of bills. Instead, they were tightly sealed, airtight compartments full of strange vials and boxes and lights. Henry thought they looked like spaceship refrigerators.

Sam blinked. This did not look like any bank he'd ever known. He had no idea what to steal, but he eyed the lasers with wonder.

Henry had seen enough adventure movies to know not to move a muscle, but Sam had not. Intrigued by his strange new surroundings, he reached out to touch a thin darting beam of light. He succeeded but recoiled with a shriek!

Flashing lights burst into action like ten thousand fire trucks, and there was a sudden noise like a million screaming cats: meee-OW, meee-OW, meee-OW, meee-OW, meee-OW! The sirens and lights split the air, and with a whimper and a wail, Sam let go of the wall and crumpled to the ground.

This was just what Henry had been waiting for.

"Home!" shouted Henry, and in a blink, he was in the field alone, standing beside a spilled bag of old coins. For a minute, he just stood, still hearing the sirens and seeing spots. Then he took a second to inspect the coins at his feet. He couldn't help it. He was curious. He picked up one of the coins and saw that it looked something like a quarter—all silvery but rough. It had a kind of lion swimming in wavy lines, and the year on the big silver coin was 1730. There were some words too. Henry felt the coin's dull surface and wondered where Zeelandia was.

Then his mind flashed to Sam, stranded in the future with the awful sirens, and he pulled himself away from the pile of money. He put his hand on the wall, took a deep breath, and shut his eyes. "Okay, wall, we need to go back to that big bank with the sirens."

Again the air was filled with the terrible screaming and the lights, but Henry didn't even need to open his eyes to find Sam. The sorry excuse for a pirate threw his arms around Henry's knees right away. He gasped and pleaded. "Please! Please! I want to go home! My head! My nerves! Smelling salts! I'm going to faint!"

When Henry did open his eyes, he saw Sam kneeling on the ground, gasping like a fish, with his eyes wide and his hands shaking. Clearly, the poor guy wasn't cut out for a life of piracy and adventure. "Sure," said Henry. "Sure. I'll take you back."

"Thank you. Bless you. I'm so sorry I ever came!"

With Sam's arms wrapped desperately around his

legs, Henry said, "Home, wall," just as the sealed round door to the vault began to open from the outside. Just in time.

Back in the field, Sam let go of Henry's legs and lay panting and crying. Henry gave him a minute while he considered how hard it would actually be to have a famous pirate villain for your father. He thought about his own parents working every day at Pearson's Pharmacy and about how they'd never even once suggested he become a pharmacist. In fact, they were very supportive of his plan to become a cowboy astronaut or a professional skateboarder.

Henry was filled with an overwhelming surge of gratefulness, and he resolved to pick up his room as soon as he got home, just to say thank you.

Once Sam was breathing normally again, he and Henry looked at each other.

"I feel bad," said Sam, hanging his head, "and what's more, I now know I'm not meant to be a pirate of any kind. This day has been interesting but so very, very stressful. I like being alone and reading my books, and that's what I'm going to do from now on. Can you please take me home?"

"We need to go get the others first," Henry reminded him.

"Oh, certainly we do," said Sam. "I feel just terrible about stranding them. I hope they aren't too angry with me!"

"And we need to take a second and return this," said Henry, nudging the bag of coins.

"Yes," said Sam glumly. "I suppose it's the right thing to do."

They put the coins back in the bag and wished themselves back to the old-timey bank, where they set the bag back on the shelf. Sam quickly returned the two bunches of bills, and it was only a matter of minutes before they were collecting Susan, Roy, and Emma, who had begun to turn a little pink in the tropical sun.

Henry was surprised the others weren't furious at Sam for stranding them. "He left you here to rot," said Henry. "Don't you care?"

"To rot?" asked Susan. "You guys have only been gone for about thirty minutes. It's hard to be mad about spending half an hour playing on a tropical beach."

"Yeah," said Emma. "I was a mermaid!"

"And I saw a shark!" said Roy. "Or a shark fin, anyway."

"Wow," said Henry. "Thirty minutes? Really? It felt a lot longer to me."

Since nobody seemed to be angry with anybody

else, they all went back to Sam's house, where he made a nice lunch of soup and bread and tomatoes from his garden. He showed the kids a shrunken head up close, and after lunch, they explored the dunes and flipped horseshoe crabs over on their backs for fun. They stopped when Susan pointed out that the crabs didn't seem to like it, but it did prove that Sam had a little villain in him after all. And the crabs seemed none the worse for wear.

At the day's end, they went home to Quiet Falls, where they made sure to turn the key before heading home.

"That," Henry said as he pedaled slowly, feeling the grit of sand in his shoes, "was not what I meant when I said the worst pirate in the world, but I guess it turned out okay."

"I'm beginning to think," said Susan, "that we won't get to control much of anything in our adventures. We seem to be at the mercy of the magic every time."

That night, when Henry was getting ready for bed, he emptied his pockets and found the coin with the lion on it. He didn't remember taking it, but however it had gotten into his pocket, he was glad. He tossed it into the air, felt how heavily it fell back into his palm, and knew—just knew—that he'd keep it forever. He set it in the back of his sock drawer in a special secret box.

A secret.

And proof.

That he had some pirate in him too.

Going Nowhere, really

THE NEXT DAY was an iffy kind of day: warm but not too hot, gray, and slightly overcast. It was the kind of weather that makes your mom or dad suggest a raincoat, but then you just end up all hot and sweaty inside it or you leave it behind someplace. Luckily, no parents were around to bother Henry, Emma, Susan, and Roy with silly things like jackets.

"Where are we going today?" asked Henry, riding his bike slowly alongside Roy on their way to the wall. Emma and Susan were pedaling behind them. "Mars?"

It was Roy's turn to wish.

Roy shook his head. "No buildings on Mars, so I think maybe we'll check out the pyramids in Egypt."

"Aw, ancient history. What do you want to go there for?" asked Henry. "Egypt's the kind of thing you do a report on for school! *National Geographic* stuff. Who wants that?"

"I do," said Roy, who was getting a little tired of Henry's attitude and who had his own subscription to *National Geographic*. "You do understand," he said, "that King Arthur is part of history too, right? So is Blackbeard."

"Well, yeah, maybe, but——"

"Besides, how can the pyramids not be cool?" continued Roy. "They're the last remaining wonder of the world. They're huge!"

"Maybe," said Henry, "but I don't see what's so great about a big triangle." He sped off, calling over his shoulder, "I guess it could always be worse. At least you aren't making us visit boring old American history!"

Looking down the road after his friend, Roy frowned, but a few minutes later, a sly smile spread across his face, and he tore off after Henry.

He was still wearing the funny smile when they arrived at the wall. He was smiling as Henry turned the key. And he didn't stop smiling as he wished. "We'd like to see some American history, a genuine pioneer building, if that's okay with you."

Then, before Henry had a chance to protest, they were all sucking in the strong smell of animals and dirt and something like oatmeal. Under their fingers was the splintery feel of unpainted wood, and above them in the rafters a dove cooed and rustled so that hay sifted down on their heads.

They were in a barn.

Henry breathed deeply and said, "Man, this place smells worse than Camelot." He sounded impressed. A goat responded by nibbling his shoe.

Susan took her hand from the wall and wiped it on her shorts. "I guess most frontier houses were on farms, so we shouldn't really be surprised, but is everything in the past smelly?"

Roy, holding his nose, answered her. "Yeah, I actually kind of think so. Indoors, anyway, since they hadn't invented air fresheners yet. If you think about it, barns in our time don't smell that great either." Just then, Emma stumbled over a chicken, and there was a great deal of squawking on Emma's part, as well as on the part of the chicken. Once Emma was standing again, everyone headed for the door. Susan pulled it open, and the kids burst through the doorway into a small fenced yard.

After the dusty dim of the barn, the gleaming day beyond was a shock. With their backs to the barn, the kids looked out at the endless prairie beyond the fence.

It was bathed in the familiar midwestern sun, wide open and alive, big and clean and honest and true. The summer day was blinding, but there was no denying that it was also absolutely breathtaking. A breeze blew past and they could hear the sound, somewhere close by, of clothes flapping on a clothesline. They stared at the prairie—flat as a sheet of paper. It reminded them of the fields near Quiet Falls, but it was much wilder. High grasses caught in the breeze, and patches of wild-flowers—pink and red and purple—were scattered randomly through the green and brown and gold of the field.

Susan said, "It's beautiful. Just like *Little House on the Prairie*."

This made Emma look up. Susan had recently given all her Little House books to Emma, proclaiming she'd outgrown them, and Emma was delighted to know this wasn't entirely true.

"I don't know, Roy," said Henry. "I still think this looks pretty boring. I mean, it's big and all, but how exciting could a prairie be?"

"This can't be it," said Roy. "If there's a barn, there's a house, and where there's a house, there must be—"

"I know!" Henry smirked. "The thrill of butter churning?"

"I was going to say 'people,'" answered Roy shortly, "but if you're determined to insult my wish and have a bad time, suit yourself!" He turned away from Henry.

This was as close as Roy came to losing his temper, and Henry felt instantly sorry. "I'm sorry, man. I was just goofing. Really—"

But Roy didn't answer because at that moment, they all heard a jingle of bells, followed by a voice calling out, "Whoa, Ginger!"

"See!" whispered Roy softly. "People!" He turned back to Henry and added, "Never mind about goofing. I've come to expect it. I know you can't help being a total doofus sometimes." He grinned, and Henry breathed a sigh of relief.

Then they heard a whip-crack, accompanied by clip-clopping. The kids turned away from the prairie and looked in the direction of the barn, which seemed to be the direction of the jingling. Because they couldn't see through the building, they all crept slowly around it until they were standing at the back of the barn.

They still didn't see any people, but directly behind the back of the barn, about twenty feet away, was the back of a little house with bright red curtains. A clothesline full of fresh linens and clothes connected the house to the barn, and clean white sheets billowed in the wind. On both sides of the little house, they saw more buildings, but like the house with the red curtains, every building faced away from the open prairie, toward the jingling and the clip-clopping and the whip-crack.

At first, the kids didn't even realize that they were looking at the back of a street, because in their minds, they'd arrived on a farm, which (in their experience) meant that they'd arrived in the middle of nowhere. But in fact, this was a town: a row of neat buildings that seemed to have been just plopped down in the ocean of grass!

This may be difficult to understand if you are accustomed to city living—the idea that a town could be so small that you might overlook it from fifty feet away, not to mention the idea that a backyard could be big enough for a barn full of animals. But this town was tiny, and the prairie surrounding it was a great empty land. (This is how almost every city begins—as a small street of shops and houses and a small group of people in the middle of nowhere. A town is really just a few buildings and a name, if you think about it.)

Cautiously, the four kids peered out from behind the house. They looked at the street and saw that the town was inviting—a neighborhood, really. People in the street stopped to talk to one another. Horses nuzzled at hitching posts.

Even so, when Susan saw the people, she sucked in her breath, grabbed Emma's hand, and ducked back behind the house where she hoped no one would see her.

"Hey!" she hissed to the boys. "Hey, get back here!"

"What's the big deal?" Henry asked, walking casually to her side. "They're just people, and they look pretty friendly."

"Whisper!" said Susan. "They may be just people, but we'll look like space aliens to them, dressed like this!" She pointed to her own silver sneakers.

But Henry wasn't paying attention. He was too busy reading a poster plastered to the back wall of the house just behind Susan's head. He pointed to it and they all turned to look.

The poster said WANTED. It had been issued in the state capital, Iowa City, and offered a whopping $5,000 reward (which seemed a lot of money, even by twenty-first-century standards) for the capture of a murderous man called "Wichita Grim."

Henry read it twice, then said (too loudly for Susan's comfort), "Okay, Roy. When you're right, you're right. This American history stuff looks fun after all! Let's check it out!" He began to walk out from behind the house, but Susan pulled him back by the neck of his shirt.

"Like I was saying," she said, "we're going to look like space aliens in these clothes." She pointed to Henry's Cubs T-shirt and then to the bright dresses and modest undergarments flapping on the clothesline nearby. "I wonder what happens to time travelers on the frontier."

They'd known they were heading for the past, but none of them had considered how they'd stand out. It hadn't mattered so much in Camelot, where Merlin had been accustomed to odd visitors, but here, on the pioneer prairie, facing a clothesline of petticoats, they knew they wouldn't be able to pass.

Glancing nervously at the window above her head, Susan crept over to the clothesline, reached up, and pulled four dresses down.

"I feel terrible," she whispered, "but I don't know what else we can do. Just try to keep them clean so that we can put them back without anyone knowing, okay?"

"But that's stealing," said Emma. "Stealing is wrong."

"We're only borrowing," said Susan, tossing a dress each at Henry, Roy, and Emma. "Unless you'd rather just go home?"

Nobody wanted that, but Henry was disgusted as

he examined his new attire. "I want pants," he said, motioning to a pair of well-worn dungarees on the line.

"Too big," pointed out Roy. "You'd look ridiculous, and people would know you'd stolen them—I mean, borrowed them."

"Plus," said Susan, "dressed as girls, we can cover up our short hair with these." She reached back to the clothesline for sunbonnets.

Henry shook his head emphatically and crossed his arms. "I draw the line."

"Fine, have it your way," said Susan, climbing into her dress. "You can wait here for the rest of us." She smoothed her hands over the long skirt and wished she had a mirror. She tied on her bonnet, tucking her hair behind her ears. "Emma, can you button my neck?"

Henry continued to groan, but with a pained expression he stepped into his dress, lost at first in the faded and flowered layers.

They were tying their apron strings when they heard a scuffling sound in the street, a commotion. Everyone glanced up sharply.

"What's that?" asked Emma.

They all peeked out into the street, a tiny packed-dirt road. From their vantage point behind the house with the red curtains, they could make out a few little stores and a handful of people, children as well as adults. They could also see that the street was clearing of townspeople, but none of the kids could figure out why.

Quickly they took off their shoes (which insisted on peeking out from under their skirts) and hid them under a rusty bucket sitting beside the house. Then they walked around the side of the house and out into the emptying street.

When they did, they saw the cause of the commotion. Barreling down the street was a cloud of dust, and at the center of that cloud of dust was a man, an enormous man in heavy boots wearing a mashed black hat that looked like it had been through a few wars and been slept in for years. The man wore a sour expression, a vest with no shirt, and guns in his belt and in his boot tops. He was coarse with stubble and grime, and he strode with purpose as the street before him cleared. People ducked into houses, slamming their doors. Even the horses looked the other way as he walked past them.

Immediately, Henry, Emma, Susan, and Roy came to two conclusions. First—that this was the man from Roy's vision, the grimy fellow Merlin had called a Saxon. And second—that this was also the murderous villain from the wanted poster on the barn, Wichita Grim!

"But," said Emma as these two conclusions sank in, "your vision was supposed to be of home."

"I know," said Roy, "and that can mean only one thing. This must be Quiet Falls!"

As the man neared, they stood holding their collective breath, as though doing so might make them invisible.

The few townsfolk stranded in the street with the kids stared in every direction except at the gigantic man. Men began fiddling with their horses' reins as women counted and recounted the eggs in their baskets. Everyone found something to do. Everyone except Henry, Emma, Susan, and Roy, who had no eggs to count, no horses to groom, and no place to go. The kids could hear murmurs all around them. "Wichita, it's Wichita Grim."

Only a cat, a big, mean-looking orange tabby, stared Wichita Grim down. Then she hopped up on a windowsill and commenced licking her paws.

The kids should have scattered when they saw him, should have run back to the barn and wished themselves home. Instead, they stared.

Why?

They couldn't help it. He was fascinating. This man was like nothing they knew in their world. Big and menacing, he chewed a cigar and scowled. They'd never seen anyone leer like that or sneer like that. He looked like a fairy-tale ogre, a villain from a cartoon or a nightmare, and he held a rope. At the end of the rope, surrounded by a second cloud of dust, was the biggest, brownest dog they'd ever seen, just as the man was the biggest man they'd ever seen. Slowly, man and dog passed, trailing the stench of unwashed criminal, dog, and smoke.

That the man did not register their wide stares is some indication of how self-absorbed a murderous villain can be. That the dog did not see them is some indication of her fear. As the kids watched, longing to liberate her, Wichita Grim turned and pulled the rope to him, hand over hand, so fast that the animal flew along the ground, despite her great size. If you think of how a piece of spaghetti flies into your mouth when you suck it in, you will have some idea of how the dog flew.

Wichita coiled and tied his end of the rope tightly to the front of a building that said SALOON and disappeared through the swinging doors. The dog sat down to lick her paws.

When the fearsome man was out of sight, Susan

crept back to the little yard beside the house. "Psssst!" she whispered, motioning for the others to follow her. This time they complied without argument.

Emma asked in a shaky voice, "Is that dog going to be okay?"

Nobody answered her.

"I said, is that dog going to be okay?" When nobody answered her a second time, Emma knew the answer. "I think we should help her," she said.

"I don't see how we can do that," said Susan. "I wish we could, but I think we just need to go home. This is a bad place to be."

Just then, in perfect punctuation to Susan's fear, a gunshot rang out in the street. The kids jumped and glanced back to see what was happening. When they did, they found that the giant man was once again standing beside the dog, but now he was holding a dark brown bottle. He'd shot off the stopper. He spat his cigar to the ground and took a long, noisy swig from the jagged neck of the bottle. Then he leaned down, pried open the dog's mouth, and poured whatever was in the bottle down her throat.

"Ain't you thirsty?" he roared as the dog choked and dribbled out a pale brown liquid. The terrible man smacked her on the head and laughed cruelly. "That's what anyone'll get who don't do what I says," he shouted in a sloppy growl. "Or my name isn't Wichita Grim!" He shot the gun into the air again, just in case there was anyone who didn't understand exactly what his name meant.

The street near the saloon had cleared completely by now. The kids huddled where they were beside the house, still as statues in their borrowed dresses. They peered out at the dog, whose eyes looked desperately afraid.

"We'd better go if we're going," whispered Susan, heading back in the direction of the barn and the prairie beyond it. "While we still can."

Henry scowled.

"I don't know," said Roy. "We saw him in my vision. Don't you think that means we're supposed to do something?"

"I think," said Susan, "that I have to draw a line at guns and murderous criminals. I'm supposed to be watching you guys, remember? I know I'm not the most experienced babysitter in the world, but I'm pretty sure I'll get in major trouble if anyone ends up—" She didn't finish the sentence. "Come on!"

Her tone was firm, so Henry and Roy finally turned to shuffle quietly after her, heading in the direction of the barn. But for Emma, who turned and took one last long look, the dog's sad eyes were like a magnet. She heard Susan's words, and though she saw the others turning to leave, she couldn't follow them. She was very afraid, but ran back into the street, trailing her good sense behind her.

Emma found herself completely alone in the street, facing down the gigantic man. Every single townsperson had found a porch to cower on or a wagon to hide behind, but not Emma. She stared deep into the villainous eyes before her. "Hey, you!" she shouted in her loudest voice. "Hey, you big, giant man—leave that dog alone, you—you—dirty SAXON!"

The man narrowed his eyes and peered at her with interest, as though he could not believe that such a little girl existed. He shook his head and looked again.

Emma ran even closer, right up to where he stood. She slipped past the giant man's feet and draped herself over the dog, who tensed but didn't move or bark.

Susan, Henry, and Roy turned and stared at Emma with their mouths hanging open. The townspeople standing on their porches froze, wondering whose unfortunate child this was. Wichita Grim, unused to being defied by anyone, much less small barefoot girls, peered down at her curiously.

He nudged her with his gun, a twisted smile at the corner of his mouth. "Aw, how sweet. Her likes the puppy." To Emma he said, "What'd you call me, little mutt-lover?"

Without raising her head to look at him, Emma said in a surprisingly firm voice, "Saxon! I called you a Saxon, and that's what you are, but I won't let you hurt this dog anymore. Untie her!"

"A Saxon?" Wichita rolled the word on his tongue, tasting it. "What's that?"

"A bad man," said Emma into the dog's matted fur. "A killing kind of man."

Wichita tossed his broken bottle aside and raised his gun. "Heh! I guess I can be a Saxon. I've been worse. I've been called Brute and Brawny and Murderer and Lout. In Wisconsin, they knew me as the Stench, and one summer in Old Mexico, I was El Diablo. Guess it won't hurt to switch it out again, keep the people guessing. Sure, call me the Saxon."

He called out to the people in the town cowering behind their doors and wagons. "You hear that, town-folk? Good people of Quiet Falls? I'm the Saxon now, and anyone who forgits it has me to reckon with. Me, the SAXON!" Then he nudged Emma roughly with his foot. "Okay. Fun's over. Get up, girl!"

Emma didn't move.

Wichita roared, "Get UP!"

Emma squeezed the dog tighter.

The dog trembled in response and made a tiny whine that only Emma could hear.

"How dares the child? This child!" roared Wichita. "Who claims this child?"

Nobody said a word, but doors began to crack open. People were watching. From where she stood beside the house, Susan reached out a hand in Emma's direction.

"You cowards!" shouted Wichita Grim into the street. To Emma he said, "People think they're better than me. These settlers all think they're the good 'uns. Go to church on Sunday, wear clean, pretty clothes, farm their fields, but when a child, a child is in danger, nobody speaks."

He shook a fist at the crowd and said, "Yer all criminals too. Everyone is a criminal. It's a bad, bad world we live in and I'm just part of it." Wichita seemed to like this idea. "Criminal world! Right, kitty?" he called out to the orange tabby sitting on the windowsill.

The cat turned away. She apparently had no opinion on the matter.

Susan, Henry, and Roy were at a loss. What could they do as long as Wichita held that gun? How could

they possibly rescue Emma in the face of that gun? Every second felt like a year. Susan thought that probably she should run up and throw herself onto Emma the way Emma had thrown herself onto the dog. She wanted to but couldn't seem to unstick her bare feet from where they were rooted beside the house.

The giant man bent over and tousled Emma's hair roughly. "Brave, stupid little girl. She's just a dog. A mangy cur. Let go of 'er and I'll spare you."

Emma shook her head and clutched the dog more tightly.

"You're such a brave one, a temper, a glorious fool. The world needs more fools. Maybe I'll just take you home with me, let you cook my beans?" He waited for her to answer, but Emma just buried her face in the dog's fur.

When she didn't answer him, Wichita reached down and grabbed her curls in his meaty fist. He pulled, and she cried out.

As soon as Susan heard Emma's cry, her feet came unglued, and she tore into the street to the very spot where Wichita stood.

"YOU!" she screamed at the top of her lungs. "You are a coward. She's six! SIX! Pick on someone your own size!" Wichita was so astonished, so thrown (and also perhaps so drunk), that he stumbled backward. In doing so, he not only let go of Emma but also let go of his gun. The gun fell and a noise exploded into the air near Susan's head.

This was just enough to finally wake the frightened townspeople of Quiet Falls. With Wichita momentarily disarmed, they ran from their homes, their porches, and the safety of their wagons. They filled the street around Susan, creating a muddle, a throng, and just enough distraction as Wichita roared and kicked his giant boots at the dog and the legs of the people for Susan to pull Emma to her feet, pick her up, and run, run, run. Hauling Emma, she dashed back to Roy and Henry, darting through the street to where they stood, still frozen beside the house.

"Run!" she shouted as she bolted past them. "Go!"

At last they turned and dashed back to the barn, tearing after Susan and Emma, who was really too big to carry and was squirming in Susan's arms.

They couldn't think about the dog anymore. Things had gotten out of hand, and they all raced past the house and clothesline and barn, and into the yard, through the barn door, and straight to their wall. There was no time to worry or breathe or return the clothes or collect their shoes.

"Wall," shouted Susan as they ducked inside, "please take us home. Home!"

It did.

In the cornfield, the kids collapsed onto the ground, panting and tangled in their long skirts. Emma finally let herself cry. She was limp and sobbing with heartache but she was also furious at Susan. "The dog!" she sobbed. "The dog. I was going to save her. How could you?"

"Gosh," Henry couldn't help saying. "Gosh, that was crazy!"

"How could you all just leave her?" cried Emma. "We aren't going to just leave her there, are we?"

Susan sat up and reached out an arm. "Em, we can't—just can't. She's only a dog. There were guns. Real guns."

Watching all of this, Roy had a sudden thought. With the others distracted, he quietly skootched over to the wall, reached out his fingers, and whispered a few careful words.

Immediately, he was back in the heart of the brawl! Only now he was on a mission.

None of the townspeople noticed him, what with all the guns firing, the hapless sheriff arriving, the yelling and the shoving, and the fainting of one large woman in a too-tight corset. None of them noticed as he blinked into view at the very front of the saloon, right next to the dog.

Roy moved quickly. In his long skirt, he knelt down, one hand still on the wall of the saloon, and stroked the dog's ear, which felt like velvet. The dog looked at him and made a tiny sound, a little moan. Roy put a finger to his lips as he pulled his pocketknife from his pocket and sawed through the thick rope.

Then he tugged on the dog's tail until a few long hairs touched the wall. The dog whined softly.

"It's okay," said Roy calmly. "We'll be home soon." To the wall he said, "Home. Home, NOW!"

And then he was back!

It had been unbelievably easy! The dog was with him and safe. He could hardly believe that it had worked, but it had, even without any planning. He grinned.

The others were all staring when Roy and the dog blinked into view. They barely had time to notice he was gone.

"Roy!" said Emma, running over. "Oh, Roy, thank you, thank you!" She wrapped her arms around his neck, and he shifted uncomfortably at the embrace but didn't stop smiling. Then Emma knelt down to pat the big bewildered dog.

"Jeez," said Henry. "I feel like a wimp. I'm the only one who wasn't a hero today. Good job, Roy!"

"No kidding," said Susan. "That was amazing."

"Thanks," said Roy. "It was actually pretty easy."

"I don't suppose you had time to get our shoes?" asked Susan.

Roy shook his head. "No, I didn't think of it. You want me to go back and—"

"No way," said Susan, laughing. "I'm sorry I brought it up. Nobody is going back into the gunfire."

"Wow, yeah, gunfire!" said Henry, shaking his head in disbelief. "That was crazy, huh?"

Roy grinned. "Yeah, it was, wasn't it? So, Henry, now what do you think of American history?"

"I stand corrected," said Henry. "I was wrong." He elbowed Roy.

"Had to happen someday," said Roy, and they both laughed.

Soap and Scissors

Now that they were all safe, they turned their attention to the dog, who was making a small but terrible sound. The dog seemed to be saying "Stay away! Help me? Stay away! Help me? Please?" Her eyes were scared. Her tail trembled. Then she looked straight at Emma and seemed to settle.

"Oh!" said Emma again. "She's big."

"Big and hurting," said Susan. "She must be, to make that noise. She looks really scared."

The dog licked one of Emma's fingers and tried to smile. She nudged a nose at Emma's knee.

"Her name is Bernice," said Emma, "and she's my dog. I know Roy rescued her, but she feels like mine." She looked to Roy, and when he offered no argument, she continued, "And now we have to fix her."

As though in agreement with Emma, Bernice let

out the smallest whimper you ever heard. It was a mouse of a sound.

"Such a tiny cry for such a giant dog," said Susan. "I wonder what the matter is." She reached over to inspect Bernice more closely, and the dog seemed pleased with the attention. But when Susan stroked one of the dog's hind legs, she accidentally pushed aside a clump of matted fur, and Bernice gave a sharp yelp. Susan flinched and pulled back her hand, but Bernice didn't nip or growl, so Susan gently pushed aside the clump of fur again.

When she did, she sucked in her breath. The leg was a mess. There was a long, jagged rip six inches long down the side of the dog's leg, clumsily mended with what looked like old string. Susan could smell the sweet ick of infection. It made her think of dirty Kleenexes.

Emma cried when she saw it, "I wonder what happened to her—"

"Wichita Grim is what happened to her," said Susan, standing up and starting to wheel her bike over to lean against the wall. "But don't worry, because now *we* have happened to her too. Come on, everyone, line up and grab your bikes. I have an idea for how to get home. I don't know why we haven't thought of this before."

They all wheeled their bikes over and reached out

to touch the wall, and then Susan wished them back home to Henry and Emma's house, because it was less likely that their parents would be there—or show up unannounced—in the middle of the afternoon. And so it was that they all found themselves on the floor of Emma's bedroom wearing calico dresses and sunbonnets, with four bicycles and one gigantic dog.

After they'd taken off their pioneer finery and hidden it in Emma's dress-up trunk, Henry ran to the kitchen for a bowl of sudsy water, a pound of lunch meat, and a bag of gingersnaps (kids need sustenance too). Emma raided the bathroom for towels and Susan dashed next door to get shoes for herself and Roy and to ransack their mother's medicine cabinet (she was a doctor, and still is). Roy just sat and stroked Bernice's ears until the others got back, marveling a little at his impulsive rescue.

When they were all back, Bernice made short work of the lunch meat (it was roast beef) and drank about half the sudsy water (it was delicious). She seemed to be feeling better, and while none of the kids was especially looking forward to it, the time had come to inspect her leg more closely.

Susan organized her armload of gauze pads, tubes, and bottles and took charge. "Emma, your job is to pet

Bernice's head and keep her distracted, but if she starts to growl, I want you to sit back, okay?"

Emma nodded, her eyes wide and wondering.

"Henry, I want you to hold her leg really still. Is that cool?"

Henry was impressed that Susan seemed to know what she was doing. He nodded his head obediently.

"Roy, you need to hold her body absolutely still, in case she wiggles. Got that?"

Roy agreed, and Susan set to work.

First she cut back the clump of matted hair so that they could see a big bald patch of white skin where the stitched and festering wound stood out like a bumpy red (and a bit yellow) mountain on a relief map. There were gobs of dried gunk all over the cut and lots of dirt sprinkled into everything, which made it hard to tell where the skin stopped and the hurt began. Susan took a towel and dripped sudsy water over the cut. With the edge of the towel, she wiped gently until the dirt and gunk began to wash away.

Bernice's leg shook, but Henry held it firmly while Emma sang softly to comfort her. "You are my sunshine. . . ."

Bernice seemed to like the song a lot.

When most of the nastiness was gone, Susan wiped

the leg clean, and the rest of the yellowish gunk came off. Although the puffy wound still looked bad, with its tangle of old string, it looked much less bad. At least you could tell it was skin. Bernice wiggled, but only the littlest bit.

Susan took a deep breath and pushed some hair out of her face. The others stared at her in admiration. "I think it'll help just to get it clean and keep the fur out of it," she said. "That way, it can scab over in a healthy way. The big question is whether we should cut out the stitches and tie it up tight with a bandage, but honestly, I'm scared to try. I'm not sure I know how to do that, and the string is pretty tangled. I don't want to pull the knots and hurt her."

Bernice looked over at Susan as if to say "Better leave it, don't you think?"

Susan poured some peroxide onto the hurt leg. It foamed and foamed, and Bernice whimpered, but Susan kept pouring and the wound kept foaming. When the peroxide ran clear, Susan gently dried Bernice's leg. She slathered the wound with ointment and wrapped the leg tightly with an Ace bandage. Finally she stood up and went into the bathroom alone. There was the sound of running water and Susan retching.

When she came back into the room, her face was

pale and dripping. Henry, Emma, and Roy clapped softly, and Henry said, "I'd like to see Alexandria do that!"

Susan blushed as she patted Bernice's head. "It's not such a big deal. I've seen our mom do it a gajillion times to Roy's knees," said Susan, but they all knew that Roy's knees had never, ever looked like that.

Bernice looked up gratefully at Susan, and then down at her leg. She gave it a stretch, testing it out. Everyone could tell she felt much better.

"So . . . what do we do with her now?" asked Henry.

"I'm going to keep her," said Emma firmly.

The other three looked around at each other and back at Emma with apologetic eyes. They knew better.

"It only works like that in books, Em. In real life, parents never let you keep a pet," said Henry, who had once found a calico cat with a litter of three kittens under the back porch. "You always have to 'do the right thing' and take it to the pound, in case it ran away from home and someone else is looking for it."

"No!" said Emma.

"Yeah," said Roy, who had briefly adopted a lost dachshund the summer before. "And while they look for the owner, your mom thinks of seventeen reasons why you can't have a pet, or she remembers she's allergic, and before you know it, someone else has adopted the animal and you never see it again."

Emma looked at Susan with fading hope, but Susan had once rescued a family of baby opossums and been forced to take them to the tiny Quiet Falls Zoo so that they could be properly reintroduced into the wild. She nodded her head in agreement. "It's true, Em. Sorry."

"Well, maybe I just won't tell Mom and Dad," said Emma. "I'll keep Bernice here in my room. I'll hide her under my bed."

"Good luck," said Roy. He glanced over at Emma's small bed and at Bernice, who was as big as the bed itself.

"Whatever we're going to do with her, I think we'd better get out while the getting is good," suggested Henry. "It'd be just our luck for Mom or Dad to swing by the house to check on us and find Bernice. We'd be toast."

"What would happen to Bernice then?" asked Emma fearfully. "Would she have to go to the pound?" Emma still wasn't quite sure what the pound was, but it didn't sound like a good thing. She pictured a place where dogs got pounded.

Since the other three kids didn't know the answer to this question, they all stood up to take Henry's advice and get out of the house while they still could. With some puffing and panting, the kids eased Bernice, now in much better spirits but still sore, down the stairs and outside into the yard, where they settled her under a dogwood tree.

Then everyone tried to think of a good place to hide her.

Henry was in favor of stashing her in a shed somewhere and taking shifts feeding and visiting her, but Susan argued that they didn't actually know of any empty sheds. Plus, she pointed out, eventually Bernice would need to go to the bathroom when one of them was not around, and that could get messy.

Roy thought that maybe the nice lady at the pet store downtown might help them, but Henry argued that they didn't really know her. "She could be a cat person," he said.

Susan didn't see why Bernice wasn't fine the way she was, sitting under a nice tree. "We can just move her to the park!"

"No," said Emma. "Someone might steal her."

The others found that idea unlikely, given Bernice's size, as well as her matted hair and funny smell, but they didn't say anything. Besides, it was probably too hot to leave her sitting outside.

Thinking of bad ideas was frustrating, and they

didn't seem to be getting anywhere, so when Emma said, "I think we should go to the library," the others didn't dismiss her entirely.

"The library?" Henry asked. "Why the library? They don't let dogs into the library."

"Bernice could have a bath in the fountain out back," said Emma. "They let dogs play in the fountain all the time, and we have to go somewhere. Besides, I like the library."

"Well, sure," said Roy. "Who doesn't?"

"Mom always says you can solve most problems at the library, and there's a lady there who's my friend. We could ask her about helping Bernice. She has to answer people's questions. It's her job."

"Which lady?" asked Susan, who was thinking to herself that the help they needed wasn't really what the help desk was intended for.

"Just someone I know," said Emma.

Emma had an odd collection of friends scattered around town, people of all ages she'd met in shops and at bus stops. They were often kooky but usually pretty nice, as grown-ups who like talking to children can be.

"She has a bun on top of her head and wears glasses," said Emma. "And she talks in a voice that sounds like a squiggly line. Like a nursery rhyme."

"Not that strange librarian," said Susan, "the one who's always gazing off over your shoulder when you ask her to help you find a book?"

Emma, whose shoulder was considerably lower to the ground than Susan's, didn't think that was who she meant.

"The one who wears her hair with a pencil stuck through it," asked Susan, "and dresses like a parrot?"

"Oh, I guess that *is* who I mean," said Emma, "but she's not strange. She's nice."

"If you say so," said Susan. "But Alexandria says that she's a weirdo, and she only became a librarian so that people would have to talk to her."

Emma looked uncomfortable at hearing such words spoken about her friend. She didn't know what to say, but Henry came to her rescue. "Alexandria is mean and dumb, and who cares anyway what someone's hair looks like? What's with you, Susan?"

Susan didn't have an answer for this. "I didn't mean it," she backpedaled, "and anyway, I didn't say she was a weirdo. I was just telling you what Alexandria said!"

Roy and Henry could tell Susan felt bad for what she'd said, but this was a cheap excuse, and Susan's meanness decided the matter in Emma's favor. While Henry and Roy would never have arrived at the library idea themselves, it seemed no worse an option than anything else they'd come up with, and at the very least, it would get the dog clean. Henry went into the garage and dug out an old red wagon, and although Bernice didn't quite fit into the wagon, they did manage to get her up onto it, though her floppiest parts spilled out.

Susan suddenly became even more helpful. She ran into her house and found a piece of rope to use for a leash, and a bottle of shampoo (no tears!). Then the kids trooped off down the sidewalk.

When they got to the library, the kids discovered that Bernice loved water. The minute she saw the fountain, she gave a normal, unhurt, happy-dog bark—the first they'd heard from her. Then awkwardly (so awkwardly that the kids made uncomfortable faces just watching) she tumble-struggled from the wagon and made a slow but straight path for the fountain, hobbling along on her hurt leg.

Thankfully, it was the kind of fountain that children are supposed to splash in on hot days, with jets of water coming straight up out of the ground. In the center of the jets was a friendly and climbable sculpture of a lady reading a book to a dolphin.

Bernice lumbered into the spray, eased her enormous self down, and rolled over onto her back. With all four legs in the air, she wiggled happily, scratching her back along the dolphin and lapping the water as it rained down.

Henry, Emma, Susan, and Roy broke into smiles of great relief.

Susan grabbed the bottle of shampoo and plunged into the fountain fully dressed. She plopped down beside Bernice, where she began to work a good lather through the dog's matted and filthy fur. She carefully avoided the hurt leg, and Bernice wiggled with pleasure as Susan's fingers tickled and scratched her belly and back.

"C'mon, guys!" Susan yelled.

Henry and Roy, who had been staring in utter shock (and delight) at Susan's madcap behavior, needed no further encouragement. They galloped into the water behind her, each taking charge of a bit of Bernice. "Man, this is the way to take a bath!" shouted Henry, running his soapy fingers through his own gummy hair.

At some point during the laughing and splashing, Emma slipped off.

And when Susan, Henry, and Roy looked up from their soapy fun a few minutes later, they found Emma holding hands with a thin blond woman wearing a bright purple dress and orange clogs. They gaped as the woman dropped Emma's hand, flashed them all a grin, and walked straight into the fountain herself. She sat down beside Bernice and stared at the dog. When she did, Bernice rolled over onto her belly and propped herself up on her front legs, facing the woman as though they were old friends. The dog barked cheerfully and licked the woman's hand.

"Hello!" said the woman to Bernice.

Bernice didn't answer in English, but the kids could tell by the way she bobbed her head that she was saying hello right back.

Then Emma walked into the fountain too. She settled herself and said, "Everyone, this is the Chirky Librarian. She's my friend. Chirky Librarian, this is everyone."

"Good afternoon!" sang the woman brightly to Henry, Susan, and Roy. She held out her slippery wet fingers and shook all of their hands very firmly and excitedly. Then she turned back to Emma and raised one eyebrow. "Chirky, Emma? What's that?"

"Cheerful," explained Emma, "and perky. Chirky!"

"Well then, okay!" said the librarian in (it must be admitted) a very chirky way. She turned back to Henry, Susan, and Roy. "It's nice to meet you," she said, "and while it's true that I am a librarian, and I'm sometimes cheerful, and perhaps also perky, you might prefer to call me Lily. It's shorter, though perhaps less descriptive."

"Okaaaay," said Susan cautiously, and thinking that perhaps Alexandria was just the least bit right about Lily.

Roy brushed water out of his eyes and Henry simply stared. Emma played happily with Bernice's tail. Everyone sat in the fountain adjusting to Lily.

"You're very . . . wet," Susan said finally.

"Thank you," said Lily. "So are you."

"You're very wet . . . for a grown-up," said Susan, trying to make herself understood.

"It happens," said Lily. She scratched Bernice behind her right ear. "I'm done with work for the day and I can do what I please. La la la." She began to sing to herself.

"Huh," said Susan. "I guess that makes sense." She smiled uneasily. Lily laughed and kept singing, and the sound was so warm and friendly that the uneasy part of Susan's smile went away. For some reason, things felt better. Maybe because what Susan had really been asking Lily was, Do you know you're kind of weird? and in her own way, Lily had answered, Yes, and isn't it fun?

In any case, nobody talked much after that. They all just sang along with Lily's la-la-la's as they finished rinsing the soap from Bernice's fur. The kids didn't

laugh and shout the way they had before, but that was okay, because you can't expect to laugh all the time, and singing nonsense songs is nice too. The day had just shifted slightly, like the weather does sometimes.

Once Bernice had shaken herself off in the sun and everyone else had climbed from the fountain and wrung themselves dry as best they could, Lily said, "I think that probably it would be best if we had some cake now. Don't you all agree?"

And since nobody ever says no to cake (unless the cake in question is very badly burned or poisoned or something else equally terrible), the kids nodded happily. They loaded Bernice back onto the wagon, and the five of them trundled off down Bloomington Street.

Lily waved goodbye to the dolphin.

Of course, Susan called her mother at work to make sure it was okay to eat cake with Lily. When you are having any sort of adventure, you have to be careful of strangers and of cake, even the kind that comes from nice librarians. But her mother, after a chat with Lily, determined that the cake in question was friendly cake, so that was okay.

Even so, Susan glanced over her shoulder nervously as she walked. At one point, she went so far as to fall be-hind the others, in a way that might be mistaken for "apart," just in case someone she knew from Quiet Falls Middle School should happen to pass by and see her trooping along, soaking wet and with a bunch of kids, a gigantic dog in a red wagon, and a strange (if chirky) librarian in a bright purple dress.

Luckily, after a minute, it occurred to Susan that the part of her that walked apart was the very same part of her that had said such mean things about Lily. It was also the very same part of her that had refused to believe in the magic in the first place, and the part of her that had gotten rid of her unicorns and her Little House books. So Susan pushed that part of herself away and ran to catch up. She put an arm around Emma's small shoulder, and when Emma smiled up at her, she was glad that she had.

From a block away, they could guess which house was Lily's. It was painted pale green and flanked on both sides by lilac trees. The front porch was purple and deliciously overgrown with honeysuckle and rambler roses. There was a windmill in the yard.

Once inside, they filed down a narrow hallway that led to the back of the house. Looking up, they noticed that the hallway's ceiling was sky blue and covered with fluffy white clouds. At the end of the hall was a red door, and when they opened it and walked into the kitchen, each of them gasped audibly. The kitchen looked like it had been transported from an old black-and-white TV show, colored all in shades of gray so that the kids in their bright clothes appeared to have been cut and pasted into an old photograph. There was a white enamel icebox, a silver table with matching chairs, a black-and-white checkerboard floor, and dishes made of cloudy white china that looked like frozen milk.

"Whoa!" said Henry.

"Yes, whoa!" Lily said with a grin, reaching into the icebox for a bottle of milk. "Isn't it fun? Sometimes I like to go back in time for a bit. Don't you?"

The kids stifled laughs at this question. They did like to go back in time—centuries back!

When Lily opened a window to toss a handful of birdseed into the backyard, the kids all stared at the yard too. Whereas Lily's front yard was freshly mown and was bordered by neat beds of flowers, the backyard had clearly not been cut in years. Not only that, the yard was enormous, surrounded by giant old trees that blocked all view of other houses. And it was full, full, FULL of wildflowers: purple coneflowers and yellow dandelions and blue chicory, like a tiny wilderness right there beyond the kitchen door.

"It's beautiful," Emma said, sighing happily. "It reminds me of the prairie we saw—"

"Really, where?" asked Lily brightly.

Henry interrupted. "She means a prairie we saw in a movie, right, Emma?"

"Yeah, right," said Emma, looking flustered. "That's what I meant—a movie."

"Really," said Lily, reaching for plates. "What movie?"

"I forget," said Emma.

"Hmmm," said Lily, but she didn't pry. Instead, she just passed out forks. And in a matter of moments, the prairie was forgotten as they buried themselves deep in slices of the thickest, tallest, most chocolaty layer cake any of them had ever seen. Nobody spoke. Everyone was content just to munch, with forks raised over cake plates, giant mason jars full of icy milk at hand, and Bernice happily lapping at a bowl of water on the floor.

"I gotta say," offered Henry at last, through a huge mouthful of fudge icing, "your house is really, really neat. I've never seen anything like it before." He swallowed and took another bite before saying, "How'd you dream all this up?"

"I'm good at dreaming," replied Lily, nudging a

large smear of frosting from her front teeth with her tongue. "But more than that, I'm just not very good at doing things the way most people do. My brain takes the way I'm supposed to do things and twists it all around like a pipe cleaner to make something else instead."

"Well, I'm glad," sighed Emma as she gazed around her. "I think it's all just beautiful. I like things to be different."

"Yes," said Lily. "But a lot of people don't like different. A lot of people work very hard to fit in."

Susan stared intently at the piece of cake in front of her.

"How's your cake?" Lily asked, noticing Susan's sudden stillness.

"Fine," said Susan, her eyes still on her plate. "It's fine."

Lily examined Susan for a second before she said, "Just fine?"

Susan shifted in her chair. "Um, no," she said, looking up. "It's great, actually. Maybe the best cake I've ever had." She searched for the right word. "It's . . . scrumptious?"

"That's very nice," said Lily. She seemed pleased. "'Scrumptious' is excellent!"

That, for some reason, reminded Susan of her old

friend Tish—of how Tish, looking up from a batch of peanut butter–banana-raisin cookies she was mixing, a book about goblins, or a dress-up trunk, would often say "Excellent!" with her eyes lit up and her head thrust forward. Susan knew Tish would never have said the cake was "fine."

"Now," Lily said when everyone finally took a break from chewing. "Tell me about this dog." She stroked Bernice, who was sitting beside her. Bernice was so big that her nose was level with Lily's shoulder. "Emma says you need my help, but why? Where did you get her? Why is she a secret? How did she get so badly hurt?" Lily looked at them all and waved a fork as she asked these questions.

Susan, Henry, and Roy fiddled with their napkins and leaned forward to answer these questions one at a time. Emma, still mildly flustered from having nearly let slip about the prairie, sat back and listened.

"We found her outside," said Henry, in response to Lily's first question.

"Because our parents will take her to the pound if they find out," added Roy, answering the second question.

"We don't really know," said Susan, in reply to the last question, "because she came that way."

Lily took all this information in and then looked at Henry. "Outside?" she asked. "Outside is a pretty big place. Where outside?"

Henry stared back mutely. "Um, hang on," he said, "I dropped my fork. Be right back!" Then he dropped his fork with a clatter and disappeared under the table to think.

While he was there, Susan swallowed the bite in her mouth, made up her mind, and decided to level with the librarian. Lily was unlike anyone Susan had ever met, but she seemed trustworthy, maybe even more trustworthy for that very reason. Lily seemed like someone who could understand the need for a secret. She seemed like a grown-up who could understand that even kids needed privacy sometimes.

"We can't tell you that," Susan said, sitting up as tall as she could, looking Lily directly in the eyes. "And we can't tell you why we can't tell you."

"Is that so?" said Lily, tapping a fudgy fork against her plate. Coming from any other grown-up, the same sentence would have sounded condescending: Is *that* so? But Lily appeared to mean just what she said. She sounded curious: Is that *so*?

This prompted Susan to offer further explanation. Her words tumbled out. "It's nothing bad," she said.

"We promise. We aren't doing anything stupid or mean. We aren't going to get in trouble. It's just that we have a . . . secret."

"A secret?"

"A secret!" Susan nodded sharply.

"Well, okay," said Lily. "If it's a real secret. Though that just makes me curiouser."

"It is a real secret," said Susan, "but even if it weren't, Bernice needs our help, no matter where we found her. If we wanted to, we could just show you a field and pretend we'd found her there. You'd never know the difference. We could lie."

"Hmmm. You make a good point," said Lily.

Susan sat back, surprised but pleased.

"Look," Henry said, "we really just need a place for Bernice to stay until we can figure out what to do with her."

Emma got up and went over to where Lily was sitting. She patted the librarian's shoulder. "Please?" she asked. "I'm going to keep her, only my mom doesn't know it yet. I need to talk her into it."

"Oh, all right," said Lily, tousling Emma's wispy hair. "I'll help you. But I'm also curious about why you came to me."

"It was kind of an accident," said Henry. "Honestly,

we just couldn't think of anywhere else to go."

"Also, I knew you liked dogs," added Emma.

"Hmph," said Lily. "I don't much believe in accidents. But that's fine. And I do like dogs. What kind of person doesn't?" She rumpled the fur on Bernice's head. "Now, who wants seconds?"

Everyone did.

Susan's Wish

THAT NIGHT, Susan couldn't go to sleep. She faced the wall, put her pillow over her head, and counted backward from 100 four times. When that didn't work, she got out of bed, sat down at her desk, and took out a piece of stationery.

The room was very quiet. No help at all. She sat back in her chair and stared at the empty piece of paper in front of her. In her best handwriting, she wrote, "Dear." But the thing about letters is that once you've got the "Dear" part out of the way, and after you've scribbled something obvious like "How are you doing?" you have to decide what to actually say. Susan tried to start her letter several times, but each time, she erased it so that the paper turned soft and pulpy under her pencil tip.

She took out another piece of paper and chewed

her pencil. "I don't have to send it if I don't want to," she reminded herself, before she hunched over and proceeded to scribble furiously for several pages. When she was finished, she folded the pages, slid them into an envelope, licked the envelope, and looked at it. It felt good, just the right thickness. You could tell, looking at it, that it was a real letter.

Then Susan got a box out from under her bed, put the letter inside for safekeeping, pulled out a scraggly, well-loved, once-white-but-now-gone-a-bit-gray stuffed bunny, closed the box, and slid it back under her bed. After that, she curled up with the bunny, shut her eyes, and went straight to sleep.

In the morning, all four kids ate breakfast together on the O'Dells' front porch and watched the neighbors leave for work. They shared bananas and bagels, the best kind of porch-swing breakfast.

"I think," said Henry with a full mouth and a smear of cream cheese on the very tip of his nose, "that all meals should be hand-holdable. I think forks and spoons should be against the law." Nobody paid any attention to this comment, as it was clearly ridiculous. How could you ever eat spaghetti without a fork? And how could you live without spaghetti?

"So," said Roy, folding his banana peel in half before laying it carefully on the table. "Where are we going today?" He looked to Susan for an answer, since it was her turn.

"Angels?" asked Emma hopefully, though she wasn't exactly sure whether they were real, and if they were, she wasn't sure they lived anywhere with walls.

"No," Henry said. "I bet we're going to Hollywood to meet a teen heartthrob!" He batted his eyelashes and pretended to faint.

"Susan wouldn't do that to us," said Roy. "Would you, Susan?"

Susan, who had been quiet all through breakfast, shook her head slowly back and forth as though she was thinking something through. She finished chewing her last bite of bagel, swallowed, and said, "No, no—of course not, but—"

"But what?" asked Emma eagerly.

"It's just, I think I want to go to . . ." Susan paused and chewed her cuticles for a minute, a sure sign she was thinking extra hard.

"Where?" chorused the others impatiently.

"Never mind," she said. "I'll tell you when we get to the wall. Speaking of which, do you think it would work to do our wishing from Emma's room? I mean, since we left it there yesterday and didn't lock the wall when we were done. Do you think we can just wish ourselves back out to the field from here? I'm kind of in a hurry."

"No dice," said Henry, shaking his head. "I already tried it."

"You what?" Roy, Susan, and Emma were shocked to hear he'd thought of leaving them out of an adventure.

"Don't all freak out. It's no big deal. I just wanted to see if it would work, so I made a wish while Emma was brushing her teeth this morning. I tried to go back to the wall. But it didn't work."

"Why not?" asked Emma.

"How should I know?" said Henry. "Maybe the wall was in a bad mood."

"Huh!" said Roy. "That's interesting. I bet the wall is time sensitive and that it only works for a certain number of hours or until sundown or sunrise or something before the magic reverts back to the field."

"Who knows," said Susan. "I don't have time to worry about it today." She hopped up from the porch swing and made for the steps.

"Why are you in such a rush? Where are we going?" asked Henry.

Susan looked back over her shoulder apologetically.

"I'm sorry, but I'm not ready to say. Let's just head out to the wall. I don't mean to be mysterious or anything. I'm just not ready to talk about it."

Before the others could say another word, Susan jumped the last two steps. Her old sandals (they were all sorry they'd left their sneakers in the past because each of them now wore flip-flops or sandals, which are far less useful for adventuring) made a big flap sound when they hit the concrete.

Everyone else followed, jumping the last two steps right behind her—even Emma, though when she landed, she landed hard, which made the flip-flopped bottoms of her feet prickle.

They all rode fast. Susan sped along because she was in a hurry to get there, and the others pedaled hard, trying to keep up. Fortunately, Emma had gotten steadier over the last few weeks, so she didn't get left behind altogether.

Still, by the time Emma got off her bike, Susan had been standing in the shade for several minutes, her hand planted flat against the stone, which was still cool from the night. She was smiling, as though whatever she'd been doubtful about was no longer an issue. Riding a bike can sometimes do just that—settle your worries.

"Come on," Susan called out happily. "If we do finish this fast, maybe we can go somewhere else afterward. I just have to give someone a letter, really."

"You know," Henry said with a heavy dose of sarcasm, "there's this thing called the mail. Maybe you've heard of it?"

Susan rolled her eyes and matched his tone. "There's this thing," she said, "called being nice. Maybe you've heard of it?"

"Sorry," said Henry sheepishly.

"Besides," said Susan, "this letter is going to one of the most famous cities on earth, and it might be fun! There's supposed to be really good pizza."

"Pizza?" asked Henry.

"What famous city?" asked Roy. "Do you know someone in Rome?"

"New York City!" Susan sang out in a theatrical voice. "The Big Apple!"

"Oooh!" said Emma, who had once gotten a postcard from her grandma, of Times Square at night, and felt like she knew something about it.

"Gangsters, at least?" Henry looked at Susan hopefully. "Old timey New York?"

"Nope, just regular old everyday today New York. Now hand over that key, Henry. Let's go."

Somewhat grudgingly, Henry forked over the key and watched as Susan fit it into the wall. "All right," he said. "But why New York?"

Everyone held out a hand to touch the wall as Susan turned the key.

Susan said decidedly, "Because that's where Tish is."

"Tish?" asked Emma.

"Yes," said Susan, "because I realized that even more than Africa or Hollywood or anything else, I just want to see my best friend. I just want to be wherever Tish is."

So . . . she was. They all were!

Nobody, including Susan herself, had realized she was wishing, so they all blinked in surprise at the unexpected change of scenery. Or lack of scenery. There wasn't much to see.

"New York is kind of dark," said Emma with a nervous edge to her voice. She looked around her at the dark walls and floor of a funny kind of basement room. There was a hum and rumbling all around them.

And it *was* dark. Or at least, this part of New York was: the underground part. There were no windows, just overhead lights that cast a strange yellow glow on everything. It was hot and muggy, and the walls were tiled like a bathroom. There were dark round spots on the ground where people had once dropped pieces of gum. Rats danced in the deep, dark ravine that ran beside them, nosing at black soot and stray soda cans.

A few people stood with them in the muggy underground place. Most of the people looked like they were in a gigantic hurry, tapping their feet and checking their watches constantly, although nothing much appeared to be happening at this late-morning hour. Other people looked as though they had no place to go at all. A man in a suit and a backpack was asleep against the wall. An old lady rode a unicycle in a lazy circle. Far off in the distance, someone played an instrument none of them had ever heard before. It sounded like a cross between a guitar and a very loud mosquito.

"This must be the subway," said Henry. "I've seen it in movies, but it's never looked so dark."

From down the ravine, which was actually a tunnel, came the sound of something—something between a chug and a clang and a swish. The sound grew louder with each passing second.

"Definitely a subway," said Henry, listening. "Definitely. I think."

The subway platform was actually very interesting, since none of them had ever been anywhere like it before. They could probably have spent a while longer examining their new surroundings, but at that moment,

Susan suddenly yelled out, "TISH! HEY, TISH!" and ran to the other end of the platform where Tish was indeed standing.

Susan made such an excited dash to see her old friend that she neglected to take note of the fact that Tish was standing with two other people. She ran on over, yelling her head off, but when she got there, she found herself facing not only her oldest, "bestest" friend in the world, who she had not spoken to in over a year, but also two strangers. Two very cool, very New York–looking strangers.

Both of the strangers had impossibly long hair, impossibly dark glasses, and impossibly pouty lips. They looked bored and beautiful in thin tank tops and chic narrow skirts that skimmed low over their hip bones—effortless. One of them had a ring in her belly button.

Tish stared at Susan with a look of sheer confusion. "Susan?" she asked in disbelief.

Susan hadn't thought about how odd her sudden arrival would seem. She had counted on Tish being alone, had imagined she'd arrive in Tish's bedroom, where she'd probably find her friend reading a book. Now she gulped and looked down, and when she did, she noticed that her own grubby shorts had a cream cheese smear on them. She felt herself blush and wondered if the wall could maybe undo all of this, take her home or maybe back in time. This was a mistake.

She looked back up and found Tish staring at her with her mouth hanging open.

"Susan? You cut your hair," Tish said, leaning forward to stare closer. "You grew! What—what are you doing here?"

And while Susan should have been thinking of a fast

answer to that reasonable question, she wasn't. Because as she stared back at Tish, she realized something. Something good! Something that trumped the belly button ring. She saw that Tish didn't look like the stylish New York teenagers. She realized that Tish still looked like Tish, with the same frizzy hair escaping a ponytail, the same dirty sneakers and freckles.

"It's a long story," Susan said, glancing nervously at the two beautiful strangers standing behind Tish. "I— umm—I'm here on a special trip. I'm here with them—" She motioned back to where the others stood, watching from a distance.

Emma waved eagerly, and Tish waved back.

"Cool!" said Tish. "But where are your folks?" She looked around the subway platform.

Susan coughed a fake cough and made a bug-eyed kind of face. A face intended to say "Can we please talk in private?" A year ago, Tish would have known right away what the face meant, but now it took her a few seconds. Then she got it and grinned.

"Oh! Oh—yeah!" She tapped the belly button–ring girl on the shoulder. "Rebecca, can I go over here with my friend for a minute?"

"Affirmative," said Rebecca. Even her voice sounded cool. "Yeah. Whatever."

As they walked a few yards away from Rebecca, Tish whispered, "Sorry about her. She's kind of my babysitter. My mom knows her mom."

"Is she a model?" asked Susan, interested in spite of herself.

"Ha!" said Tish. "She wishes. No, she's just a dumb teenager, not nearly as cool as she looks. Her mom calls her Becky-boo." Tish rolled her eyes. "The sad thing is that I help her with her homework."

"That's no fair," said Susan. "You have to have a babysitter *and* do extra homework?"

"I know," said Tish. "I'm sooo embarrassed. I mean, I'm twelve, but my folks say the city isn't safe for me to be alone in." Tish sighed. "She's totally bleckish."

Susan laughed. "Bleckish" was a secret word that Tish and she had invented in the fourth grade as part of their secret language. Susan felt a warm rush of memory and knew everything would be okay—everything! She stopped walking and turned to her friend. "I missed you," she said. "I missed you a lot!"

"I missed you too!" said Tish excitedly. Then her face fell and she looked hurt and angry. "But—if you missed me, why didn't you ever write me back? I e-mailed you three times before I gave up. I even sent you a postcard, just in case I had your e-mail address wrong."

"I know," said Susan, looking down to avoid Tish's gaze. "It was terrible of me. I wish I could say that I didn't get the e-mails or the postcard or that I forgot or something. But I have to tell you the truth—and the real reason is even worse, if you can believe that." She made an effort to make eye contact, but it was hard.

"What is it?" asked Tish.

Susan planted her feet on the subway platform and gritted her teeth. She closed her eyes and said, "It's awful, and if you're mad, I understand, but see—at first I was mad at you—"

"You were mad at me?" Tish clearly found this idea preposterous.

Susan opened her eyes. "I guess so, yeah, for leaving me. I was so lonely—"

"You were lonely!" said Tish. "You think *you* were lonely? You have no idea. At least you were still at home with your brother and the O'Dells. I was here . . . with people like that." She motioned to Rebecca. "All by myself!"

"I didn't think about it like that. I thought that you were having an adventure. I felt . . . left behind."

"Oh," said Tish morosely. "I guess that makes sense, kinda, but you were wrong. I mean, New York is cool, but my parents don't let me go anywhere, and school didn't start for a long time, so I didn't meet anyone for months. I was all alone. It was like being grounded. I didn't tell you that, so I guess you didn't know, but still, you should have written back."

"I know," said Susan. "I was awful, but that's not even the worst part. The worst part is that after that, I made new friends. And I was sort of . . . distracted. I just kind of forgot about you. About me too, I guess."

"What do you mean?" asked Tish. "How could you forget yourself?"

Susan gulped. "The new friends, they're different, and I started to feel different too." She scuffed her grubby sandals against the filthy floor and made a big, new dirty spot on her big toe. "I started to feel older and cooler. And the things we used to do together seemed . . . young and babyish. I felt like I'd outgrown them—and you—and maybe even me."

Tish looked sad.

"It's so dumb!" said Susan. "I can't believe I was so dumb. I don't even like my new friends very much. They're mean. Do you think—do you think you can ever forgive me?"

"What friends?" asked Tish suspiciously.

"Alexandria Lenzi." Susan winced as she said it.

"Alexandria?" Tish stared in disbelief. "She doesn't

like books! She brings diet soda in her school lunch!"

"I know," said Susan glumly.

"Ugh," said Tish, thinking things over. "She's pretty terrible."

"I know." And Susan did know it, now that she had a real friend in front of her. "I'm so sorry! But she was nice to me—sort of. She let me sit with her in the cafeteria, and it was better than being alone."

Tish wrinkled her nose.

But Susan went on. "And then, when I began to really miss you, when I wasn't angry anymore or distracted, it was too late. I'd already not written so many times. When the postcard came, and I knew you were angry at me, I didn't know what to say. I just kind of made myself forget you. I threw away the postcard and deleted the e-mails."

Tish looked very hurt.

"But, Tish, I'm sorry. I can't forget you. Nothing is the same since you left. Everyone at school only wants to talk about boys and hair and nail polish."

"That sounds really boring," said Tish.

"It is," agreed Susan. "And you know what else? I put all the things—all my real things—away. My unicorns and books and everything. But it kind of felt like—like I'd put me away, put myself away too. And

I know—I know I need to grow up, but there has to be a fun way to do it, right? I don't want to outgrow the stuff that's the most fun. I don't want to forget me anymore. Or you."

Tish took all of this in but said nothing. She seemed at a loss for words. Susan waited. Out of the corner of her eye she could see the other kids standing back. Henry was tapping an imaginary watch and she feared he'd come over if they didn't finish soon.

"Tish?" Susan asked nervously.

"Yeah," said Tish. "That's pretty awful, because I really needed you. *I* was the one who'd gotten stuck in this big new place, and everyone else was so cool and everyone seemed taller than me and I had to have a sitter. A babysitter!"

"I know," said Susan. "I'm so sorry. I wrote you a letter last night and tried to explain all of it, but now I've said everything." She took the letter from her pocket.

"I'll take it anyway," said Tish, grabbing at the envelope. "*I* save letters."

"So now I guess I'm bleckish too, huh?" asked Susan. "Like Alexandria?"

"Yes," said Tish, knitting her brows. "You most certainly are." But she smiled. "Fortunately, you're more

202

swizzkilydoo than you are bleckish, so it's okay. You're lucky I'm a very forgiving kind of person."

Susan looked relieved. "You are," she said. "You're the best kind of person in the world!"

Tish moved to hug her friend, but Susan put up a hand to stop her. "Wait!" she said. "There's just one more thing I have to confess."

"There's more?" Tish looked incredulous.

"Yes, but it's a little thing," said Susan. "I just need you to know that while I think diet soda is dumb and books are the best, I don't exactly hate fashion magazines and I do kind of like nail polish, especially the sparkly kind."

"Well, yeah!" said Tish, laughing. "It looks like magic, like fairy dust! Just wait until you get your first New York manicure. They can paint flowers on for you!"

And then the girls hugged.

After that, Tish said, "Okay, so this is great, and it's awesome to see you, but I'm confused. I still don't understand. Where are your folks? Why are you here?"

Susan stammered. "I—um—I can't tell you."

"What?" Tish said. "Why not?"

Susan looked uncomfortable. "Wait, can you hang on a second?" Before Tish could answer, Susan ran over to the others, who were loitering not far away.

Maybe the others would have been more obstinate about holding to their sworn oath if they were not standing on a hot subway platform, waiting to begin their next adventure. But under the circumstances (and given that Tish had been a friend to all of them for years), they caved. In a matter of seconds, Susan was back with the others in tow and a huge smile on her face.

"Okay," she said eagerly. "Are you ready for a secret?" she asked. "A big, big, BIG secret? The biggest, most magical secret EVER?"

Tish nodded vigorously, her face alight and expectant.

But suddenly there was a thunderous noise. All in a moment, there was a blast of heat and a rush of metal, and the subway slid into the station. The doors opened and people spilled out. Rebecca called for Tish to follow her and disappeared with her friend through the next set of doors.

This all happened very fast.

"Come with me?" Tish begged as she ran over to the train and stood at the door, waiting to see what Susan would say. She beckoned wildly and called, "Please come! I want to know the secret! I want to see you!" She flailed her arms so wildly that she almost knocked over a jaunty blond teenage boy in a blue T-shirt who happened to be standing beside her.

And Susan, who couldn't help noticing the jaunty blond boy, did just as Tish asked. She ran over, jumped aboard, turned, and called out, "Come on, guys!"

Henry followed immediately, and leapt in with a loud thunk, just as the blond boy regained his balance and straightened his sunglasses.

"Get on," Susan yelled to Roy and Emma nervously. They were moving more slowly than Susan and Henry. "Get ON! Hurry!"

They didn't hurry fast enough, and the doors slid shut, almost catching Emma's nose. Roy and Emma were stuck on the outside of the subway car! Tish, Henry, and Susan stared at them through a pane of scratched glass.

"Wait!" yelled Roy, banging on the window. "Let us in!" But it was too late.

The train took off down the tunnel.

Just. Like. That.

Brooklyn Bound

INSIDE THE SUBWAY CAR, Henry turned to Susan, furious. "Now what do we do?" he asked. "Bad enough we didn't get to meet any mobsters or King Kong or anything, but now we've left Roy and Emma behind!"

"Mobsters?" Tish looked interested. "What mobsters?"

Susan was aghast. "Henry's right. We have to go back!"

"Wait!" Tish exclaimed. "King Kong? What *is* the big secret?"

"Hold on, Tish!" said Susan. "We just lost Roy and Emma! We have to go back——"

Tish shook her head. "There's no way to do that, really. We can get off at the next stop and wait for a train heading back the other way, but this is an express line, so we won't stop for a while, and there's no telling how long it would take to catch the return train at this time of day. It'll be at least twenty minutes before we can possibly get back to them, and by that time, they might be gone. Won't they just get on the next train?"

Susan considered this. "I doubt it," she said. "They won't know where to get off. Can we call them? Can we call the station?"

"No," said Tish. "There's nobody to call. New York is really different from Quiet Falls."

Susan looked miserable.

"But you know," continued Tish, "I bet they'll figure out how to board the next train and ride it to the end of the line."

"How would they know that?" asked Henry.

"Just considering where this train is going," said Tish.

"Where's that?" asked Susan.

Tish grinned and pointed at the sign above her that read CONEY ISLAND.

And while Susan and Henry still felt sick to their stomachs, there wasn't much they could do until they got to where they were going. Hoping desperately that Tish was right, they found themselves seats and told Tish all about their wall. About Merlin, and Sam, and Wichita Grim, and Bernice the dog, and even the blond boy from Susan's glimpse, who had turned his back on them and was talking to a friend.

"Why did you see him when you said the word 'love'?" asked Tish excitedly. "You think you're going to fall in love with him?" She stared at his back in wonder.

"No, goofball." Susan elbowed her friend. "I thought I was seeing him, but I wasn't. Obviously, I was seeing you, only I was so distracted by him that I didn't even notice you were in the vision!"

"Oh," said Tish. This was complimentary but not nearly as romantic or interesting. "Okay!"

Another subway platform flashed by.

"And where's the dog now?" asked Tish.

"She's with this librarian friend of Emma's," said Susan. "You might know her. Her name's Lily, and she wears superbright colors."

"Sure, I remember her," said Tish. "She's cheerful, right?"

"Emma calls it chirky," Henry laughed.

"Yeah," said Susan. "I used to think she was weird, but she's not. Or she is, but in a good way."

"Do you think your parents will let Emma keep her—the dog, I mean?" asked Tish.

"Nah," said Henry. "Mom really hates dogs, but I bet Lily will adopt her. She really seems to like Bernice, and Bernice likes her. Don't you think, Susan?"

"Maybe," said Susan. "That's usually what happens in books, isn't it? The magic creates a problem but it solves the problem too, right?"

They all agreed that this was usually the case, and Susan made a mental note to herself that they all should go check in with Bernice and Lily after dinner, just to see how things were going.

Tish changed the subject. "Hey, maybe Roy and Emma don't even need to figure out the train. If they have the magic wall with them, can't they find us? Can't they just wish themselves to where we are?"

"Ooh! Let's hope they think of that," said Susan.

"It'll be fine," said Tish, settling happily into her seat. "They'll figure it out. They've both done it before."

Susan still felt worried, but just then the train rose up out of the ground and ran onto an elevated rail over Brooklyn. Down below them were houses and people and streets full of cars and walls painted with colorful graffiti. To Henry and Susan, who had spent their lives in Quiet Falls, this was almost as interesting as the quiet tropical cove, the blazing frontier prairie, and even the dark stones of Camelot, because as different as Brooklyn was from Quiet Falls, it was still part of their world, the world of today. This city, New York, was huge and bustling and colorful and exciting and different from anything they'd ever seen, but unlike Camelot, if they wanted to, they could live here someday. They could visit without magic, and that was pretty neat.

"Wow!" said Henry, staring at the buildings that went on for miles. "It's really big."

"Yeah!" said Susan, putting a hand to the window and pointing at all the cars going past. "Just one of those buildings has, like, an entire town in it."

Then she looked down the length of the subway and couldn't help noticing a man several feet away who looked like he'd come from some magical past himself. He was wearing a black dress, an ornate silver necklace, and a black headdress. He sat peering over his long gray beard, reading a book of what looked like magical runes. He looked up and smiled, gave a little wave, and went back to his book.

On the man's right, a large woman in a flowered dress and a straw hat fanned herself with a magazine, and on his left, a boy with a green Mohawk listened intently to a set of headphones.

"Wow," said Susan. "Wow."

"Yeah, it's pretty interesting," said Tish. "But just wait for Coney Island."

Meanwhile, back on the subway platform, Roy and Emma sat calmly, thinking that surely Henry and Susan would come back for them. Roy read a newspaper he found on the bench beside him while Emma wandered over to a snack counter, where a very nice man with an accent tried to sell her a gigantic cookie half frosted with chocolate icing and half with vanilla.

Emma didn't have any money, so she left the counter and tried to strike up a conversation with a nice-looking lady sitting on a bench and reading a book. But the lady must have been at a very interesting place in the story, because she simply ignored Emma and scooted over farther on the bench.

This drew the attentions of a second lady, who bustled over and called Emma "You poor little thing" before offering to "report" her. Emma wasn't sure what this meant exactly, but it didn't sound very nice, so she backed away from the woman and returned to Roy on the bench.

As she climbed up beside him, Roy set down his paper and looked at Emma. "I don't think they're coming back for us," he said. "I think we need to go."

"Where?" asked Emma.

"Somewhere," said Roy.

Emma nodded silently.

"Let's think a minute," he said, scratching his head.

Emma nodded. "Okay." She tried to think very hard, and scratched her head too.

This was tricky, as both Roy and Emma were used to being bossed around. Although both of them were perfectly capable, smart, and resourceful, neither was accustomed to taking the lead. Still, Roy enjoyed problem solving, and this was an interesting conundrum. Emma's rapt attention spurred him on.

"Let's consider all our options," he said, "since we only have a few. We can take the train, we can go aboveground, or we can use the wall. I'm going to suggest that we not go aboveground, since that's the one place in New York we know Henry and Susan are not."

This made good sense to Emma. She nodded.

"In that case, we can either take the train or the wall," continued Roy. "If we take the train, we're headed in the right direction, but we don't know where to get off. If we take the wall, we might leave the others behind if they do come back. Hmm." He pondered the choice.

"We have to take the wall," Emma said, "because if we don't take it with us, it'll get stranded here, and we'll all be stuck in New York. Forever!"

"Huh!" said Roy. "I hadn't thought of that."

"Also," said Emma, "it's faster, and we can just go

home for a minute and then wish ourselves to wherever Henry and Susan are!"

"Hey, that's right," said Roy. "Good use of logic, Em! We can do what you did in Camelot, can't we?"

Emma nodded proudly.

So they headed back over to the tile wall and touched it gingerly (it was very dirty), and Roy said, "Home, please!"

Although the lady reading the book was still sitting nearby on the platform as they blinked away, she didn't notice a thing. It must have been a very good book!

Emma and Roy were greatly relieved to find themselves back in the familiar field, with a gentle summer breeze blowing across their faces and the sun shining hot on their heads, but they didn't have time to enjoy it. They kept their hands on the wall, and Emma said right away, without thinking, "Okay, Mister Wall. Now we'd like to go to where Susan and Henry are, please! To the train."

But nothing happened.

Roy wasn't surprised. "Honestly, I didn't think it would count as a building," he said. "We'll have to think of another way."

Emma frowned. "Like what?"

"Hmm. We don't know where they're going, so we

can't go to wherever that is and wait for them to get there. But maybe—could we wish to be where they're going . . . in the future? The same way we went to Quiet Falls in the past? Could we wish to be with them in an hour? Let's try!"

Emma nodded, and they both touched the wall as Roy said, "We want to be with Susan and Henry, in the building they're in, at lunchtime today!"

And sure enough, there they were! In a place that smelled more like hot dogs than either of them thought possible. A few feet away, Tish sat staring at them, with a hot dog in her mouth. She almost choked. She pointed and made a sound like glachgh!

Henry and Susan whipped around, ran over, and hugged them with hot dogs in their hands.

"All riiiight!" shouted Henry, slapping Roy on the back. "You did it!"

"It wasn't so hard," said Roy. "It just took a little figuring out."

"I used logic," said Emma proudly. "Roy's teaching me!"

Susan beamed and patted their heads, Tish wrapped both of them in a big bear hug, and Rebecca the baby-sitter and her equally beautiful friend didn't notice a thing. They weren't really paying attention, which is the way it is sometimes with teenagers.

After Susan, Henry, and Tish told Emma and Roy about the things they'd missed (which included a wooden roller coaster that had made Susan's head hurt), Roy and Emma explained how they'd found the group by going slightly—just slightly—into the future.

"Wow. This is the future?" said Henry, remembering the liquid-looking walls of the high-security bank vault he'd visited with Sam. He looked around and said, "It looks pretty much the same to me. Does it feel any different to you?" Then a thought struck him. "Wait, do you need to go back?" he asked.

"I don't think so," said Roy. "Do we, Emma?"

Emma shrugged.

"I mean, if we all went back in time," said Roy, "we'd just be stuck in the subway again, and if we went further back, then this morning would never have happened. I think it's better to just stay where we are."

"But does that mean you lost two hours of your life?" asked Tish.

Emma was horrified by this idea until Susan pointed out that they regularly lost hours of their lives: whenever they took naps, or watched really, really, really bad TV. This made the missing time seem less frightening, so they finished up their hot dogs and headed out to the boardwalk.

A BRIEF NOTE
ON THE TRUE NATURE
OF (FUN AND) DISASTER

*P*erhaps you've noticed in books like this one that every wish seems to result in a chase or a fire, or an important and potentially disastrous event or discovery of some other kind. And perhaps you've thought to yourself (because you are clever), "Yeesh! If I found a magic talisman, I'd avoid all that mess and just go to Disney World!"

Well, there is something you need to understand. For some reason, writers like to leave out the regular parts of a magical tale, probably because plain old good fun is not especially dramatic or exciting. This is silly, but it's just something writers do.

Most writers are show-offs and they like lots of drama. Even me.

But in the name of absolute honesty, I'm now going to tell you something that I might otherwise have left out. I'm going to share with you that the four kids did, in fact, have a fabulous time with Tish on the boardwalk. They had fun because there were lots of new things to see and interesting people to stare at. There were bumper cars and a tattooed lady who walked past carrying an enormous snake. There was a one-man band, and a group of fire-eaters and jugglers, and they found post-cards to buy and ridiculous hats to try on. They had fun because it was an adventure, they were on their own, the magic had brought them, and because Tish, who had been lonely for a year, was very, very glad to see her best friend again.

They walked down by the water too, where Susan and Tish helped Emma built a sand castle while Rebecca and her friend sat on the beach and looked beautiful. And when the blond boy from Susan's vision just happened to walk by with a pack of friends, and he just happened to drop his sunglasses at Rebecca's feet, and then he just happened to strike up a conversation with Rebecca, Susan didn't mind a bit.

They ate funnel cakes, drank lemonade, and played Skee-Ball (which the blond boy—whose name turned out to be Gavin—was very good at, though winning isn't really the point of Skee-Ball), and at last the day was over and Susan and Tish hugged and whispered promises to see each other again soon and to e-mail and call. And then it was time to go home.

Which they did.

Yes, they all made it back safely, without even the most minor of minor mishaps.

They had been gone for hours, and nobody had chased

them, except a seagull who wanted a bite of Emma's funnel cake. They hadn't gotten lost, frightened, or caught. They hadn't been separated again, and they found the wall right where they had left it, in the room full of hot dogs.

They made it back to the field safely, locked the wall for the night, and were home in time for dinner. With seconds to spare.

No, nothing bad happened at all. It was a fun afternoon and free of all disaster, and it didn't affect anything that happened afterward, not even a little. In fact, I wouldn't bother to include this particular adventure in the book since it doesn't matter much to the story.

Except that it does. Because fun does matter. It matters a lot.

The End (or something like it)

THE NEXT DAY, Henry, Emma, Susan, and Roy woke to the sound of rain. And while rain is a wonderful sound to wake to (far pleasanter than an alarm clock or your mother yelling that breakfast is getting cold), each of them, in their separate beds in their separate rooms, groaned aloud and went back to sleep in hopes of a sunny afternoon.

If the rain had come a few days earlier, they might have climbed out of bed anyway and biked to the wall in the storm, but now, spoiled by a number of magical adventures, slightly sunburned, and filled with pleasant memories of Coney Island, they were willing to wait for sunshine.

This is why Susan and Roy were still in bed when the phone rang at 10:07 a.m. and why they were still in bed when it rang again, and kept ringing, at 10:17 a.m.

Roy finally got up to answer it on about the twentieth ring. He groaned, "Hello?"

"Come over, now," Henry said, and he hung up just as Roy was opening his mouth to ask why.

Roy woke Susan and they brushed their teeth hurriedly, tossed on some clothes, and ran next door. They were in such a rush that despite the torrential downpour, they didn't bother with umbrellas. But even so, they couldn't miss seeing the incredible car parked out in front of the O'Dells' house. It looked like a small schoolbus had gotten mixed up with a coffee table. It was something called a woodie (though the kids didn't know to call it that), and it was cool!

They burst through the front door, shaking off water and yelping. Roy shouted out, "Did you see that car!" before they noticed Lily and Bernice in the living room. Lily was sitting on the couch in a startling bright turquoise slicker with pink polka dots. Bernice looked like a furry mountain at her feet.

"So, you like my car?" asked Lily brightly. "I like it too! Maybe you'll come for a ride later."

"Lily!" said Susan. "We were going to come over today to see you and Bernice. I promise! But it rained and—"

"Yes," said Lily. "Mmmmhmmm. Rain does make

for good snoozing. I forgive you. But when I didn't see you guys yesterday, I figured I'd pop by today and check in. Bernice wanted to say hello. She's such a friendly girl."

When Bernice heard her name, she looked up and grinned . . . or panted. It was hard to tell which.

Lily reached over and patted her head. "Such a good, good girl," she crooned.

Susan flashed Henry a look, and he grinned back. Everything was coming together just as they'd hoped it would.

"She *is* a good girl." Emma beamed. "Don't you just love her so much?"

"Yes, I do. She's wonderful. But as wonderful as she is, I have to go out of town in a few days, so we need to figure out what to do with her."

"What do you mean?" asked Henry. "Aren't you going to keep her?"

"Why would I want to keep her?" asked Lily, sounding taken aback.

"Yeah," said Emma, who had not been privy to Henry and Susan's conversation on the train, "why would Lily keep her? She's my dog, and just as soon as Mom and Dad—"

"It's never going to happen," said Henry in his

kindest, most good-brother voice. "You have to understand that, Emma, and Lily might be the best chance Bernice has!"

Lily shook her usually chirky head in a sad way.

"But dogs are good for protection?" suggested Roy. He got down on his knees and crawled across the floor to look Bernice in the eyes. "And walking her will be really good exercise." He tousled the dog's head and looked up at Lily.

"Yes, that's all true," admitted Lily, "but still—I only said I'd watch her for a day or two while you came up with a plan. Heavens, I can't keep her for good!"

"Are you allergic?" asked Roy. "My mom is allergic, and that's why we can't have a dog. Or at least, that's what she says." Roy considered thoughtfully that he had never actually seen his mother sneeze, wheeze, or itch in the presence of a dog. He'd have to ask about that.

"Nope," said Lily. "I'm not allergic to Bernice at all. I'm just too busy."

Emma looked confused. Although she didn't want Lily to keep Bernice forever, she knew deep in her heart that Henry was probably right, and in any case, she thought the librarian should *want* to keep Bernice. "But you love dogs!"

Lily chuckled and stroked Bernice's head, which

was in her lap. "I do love dogs, Emma, but I always *have* loved dogs, and you don't see me with any other dogs, do you? Don't you think if I wanted a dog, I'd have one already?"

"This is different!" said Emma. She cocked her head as she thought this over. "Bernice is special."

"Dogs are a lot of work, and I'm gone all day. I travel a lot to library conferences and book fairs. It wouldn't be fair to Bernice. Or to me."

"To you?" asked Susan.

"Yes, dogs are hard work," said Lily. "Why, just in the last twenty-four hours, she's eaten a few house-plants and chewed up the legs of my favorite chair."

"Oh!" said Emma, who felt responsible. "I'm sorry!"

"Don't be," said Lily. "I agreed to watch her for a bit, and I've had a nice time walking her and cuddling, but now I'm done. So"—she held Bernice's leash in the air—"what now?"

They hadn't prepared for this at all. Henry, Roy, and Emma turned to Susan, who usually had an answer for everything but was now silent.

"Come on, guys," said Lily, shaking the leash. "I'd love to keep her, but I just can't. It isn't practical for me just now. Maybe someday . . ."

Susan cleared her throat. "But, Lily, *you* aren't

practical. I mean, you don't have to take the dog, but this doesn't sound like you. It sounds like something a real grown-up would say."

"I *am* a real grown-up, Susan," said Lily, setting down the leash. "I'm thirty-three years old. I have a PhD in library science and a good job. I own a house, a car—"

"A nice one!" said Henry appreciatively.

"Thank you," said Lily, smiling at him.

Susan shook her head. "But you aren't a regular grown-up. Your house is different. And your car is different. And your hair is different."

Lily felt at her bun, which was, today, held together with two forks. They were jammed in so that the tines faced out.

Susan continued, "Real grown-ups don't have prairies in their backyards or wear forks in their hair. That's not practical either."

Lily sighed. "You aren't alone in thinking so, Susan. People have been saying things like this all my life, but they're wrong, and so are you. How I wear my hair is not really an issue of practicality at all. What difference does it make?"

Susan looked at her feet.

"I make choices based on how I want to live, just

like you do," said Lily. "I may eat soup for breakfast or wear slippers to the grocery store, but those choices are completely separate from my adult responsibilities.

"I may paint my house a funny color, but I keep it clean. I may turn my backyard into a prairie, but I mow the front yard because I don't want neighborhood kids cutting through it and getting ticks. I can choose to sleep in the afternoon and dance all night, precisely because I *am* a grown-up, but I can't choose to be able to take care of Bernice right now, because I don't have the money or the time. And I can't choose to have more time and money, though I wish I could. No—she'll be better off at the pound where someone who does have enough time and money will come and adopt her."

"NO!" shouted Emma, her eyes welling with tears.

Lily turned to Emma, reached out, put an arm gently around her, and said, "Emma, have you ever been to the pound? In some cities, it's a brutal place, but here in Quiet Falls, it's quite nice. I volunteer over there on weekends when I have time, in the Cat Room. You can come along sometime if you want, to visit Bernice."

"The Cat Room?" Emma's voice shook, but she couldn't help being interested.

Lily gave her a squeeze. "It's a wonderful place. There are anywhere from fifteen to twenty cats who live there at a time, and they all play and cuddle together in one room. There are toys and towers and beds for them, and people like me go spend the day with them. Or you can take the dogs out to play in the yard—"

"I'd like that," said Emma.

"Well, how about you and I take Bernice over there right now, and we'll play with the cats. Then, maybe once a week, until Bernice finds a home, I'll drive you over there to see her. How would that be?"

Emma nodded, but only a little. She still wasn't quite sure.

Lily stood up, reached for a bright red umbrella, and held out her other hand. "Who wants to come for a ride?"

Roy and Henry jumped to their feet, but Susan raised a hand. "No thanks," she said. "I don't mean to be ungrateful, and I'm sorry about what I said before, about your hair, and—stuff. But I have another idea."

The others looked surprised but fell back to listen.

"You do?" asked Emma.

"Yes, I do," said Susan.

"Susan, I really don't mind helping," said Lily.

"No," said Susan. "Thank you, but I think that this is my responsibility. I was supposed to be in charge, and so it was my decision to bring Bernice home with us.

I thought you would step in and handle it, but really, it's my job. Now I think I may have a solution."

She arched her eyebrows meaningfully at the others.

"But it's raining," said Henry. "And Bernice is still limping pretty bad, and Lily's car—"

"Suit yourself," said Susan. "You can go in the car, but I've got something else to do."

Henry grumbled. Roy looked as though he wanted to grumble. Emma waited for someone to tell her what to do.

When it became clear that nobody was going to join her, Lily said goodbye chirkily and left with no hard feelings, because although she was indeed a real grown-up and had to wonder about their secret, she was also a kindred spirit and a friend.

After she was gone, Susan picked up Bernice's leash and grabbed her own yellow raincoat off the coat tree by the door. "Who wants to come to the wall?" she asked.

Rain or no rain, everyone did.

Walking in the rain was no fun.

They couldn't ride their bikes because they had to pull Bernice in the wagon, since it was too far for her to walk on her hurt leg. As a result, the hour-long hike out to the field took even longer than usual. The wet pavement under their feet made for slippery footing, and each time a car went past, they all had to jump off the road into a streaming culvert, so they got drenched. Raincoats made almost no difference, and although it was summer, the water was cold enough to make their teeth chatter. As they marched through the field, their knees bumped the cornstalks, which made things even worse. For the first time, the magic seemed like a chore.

Silently they moved toward the wall. Silently they placed cold hands on the chilled stones. Emma wheeled Bernice over to the wall too, and when she held the dog's tail out to the wall, she could feel Bernice shivering beneath her heavy, wet fur. Henry and Roy were whispering about something as Henry fitted the key into the wall and turned it. This made Susan nervous.

"Don't you go making any wishes!" she cautioned.

"Wait a second," said Henry, who had not been thinking about wishes but didn't like to be told what to do. "How come you get a wish today? You had a wish yesterday, and you wasted it on boring old New York." (This was unfair of him, since he'd had a great time in New York, but when you're in a grumpy mood and have been forced to march in the rain, it's easy to be unfair.)

With a wave of her hand, Susan dismissed him. She turned to the wall and said, "Wall, we'd like to go back to Camelot, to see Merlin again, please?"

Then the rain was gone and they were all back in Camelot, in the pig yard just beyond the door to the lean-to. Only now it was a sunny day in Merry Olde England. There were birds tra-la-la-ing, darting around, and picking berries from a hedge along the courtyard wall. The queen was singing as she caught butterflies with a net, and though Emma hated to think of what the butterflies were for, Guinevere made a lovely picture dancing across the lawn. The packed dirt beneath their feet was full of soft shoots of new grass. Off in the distance, they could hear the clatter and crash of two knights practicing the art of friendly swordplay, and from each tower in the castle, colorful flags rippled in the breeze.

Henry pushed back the hood of his jacket and squinted up at the sun. "Okay, okay. Maybe this was a decent idea after all."

Roy took off his coat, ran a hand through his wet hair, and pointed to an animal eating from a trough. "Hey, is that a unicorn?"

The animal started, as though it recognized the word. It raised its head and turned to look over at them. Everyone gasped. It was, indeed, a unicorn. Sort of.

It didn't look iridescent and magical, the way unicorns usually do in pictures, all glowy and white. Its mane was not silver. It did not have big blue eyes fringed with thick lashes.

Really, the unicorn looked most of all like a wild pony. It was a soft brown color, tightly muscled, and dark-eyed. It looked like an animal that might grace the cover of a horse book, except that from the center of its forehead rose a long tusk of sorts, a yellowish piece of bone that ended in a very sharp point. The horn (if you could call it that) looked like a weapon, and the beast looked like a gentle and loving creature, so the overall effect was odd. Imagine a deer with antlers made of razor wire and you'll have some idea of the effect. His eyes made the kids want to pet him, but his horn was a warning.

Susan stared and held her breath, and Emma clapped her hands with delight. They were all so awestruck as to be oblivious to everything else, until Bernice gave a big shake and sent a torrent of wet dog water over each of them. The unicorn made a snorting noise, shook droplets of water from his head, and resumed eating.

From the lean-to came Merlin's voice. "I'm up! I'm

up, I tell you! I've been awake for an hour, Jeffrey. No need to snort. I've got an apple for you right here, if you'll only wait a second!"

The wizard stepped through the door, wiping his face with a rag, and took note of the four of them and the great wet dog too. He said, "Oh, hello, children! I've been sleeping, as you well know. Good morning! Good morning!"

When he lifted away the rag, they all gasped. His beard was gone!

"But—but—you can't shave your beard!" said Emma. "You're Merlin."

"So what?" asked Merlin. "You don't have a beard. Why do I have to have one all the time? Hot and itchy it is, and whenever I eat jam, it gets simply full of bees. It's spring, and if the sheep can be shorn, why not old Merlin?"

"Because you have to have a beard," explained Henry. "Nobody ever thinks of Merlin without a beard."

"Except everyone who ever knew me as a boy," said Merlin. "You think I was born with a face like a stickle-bush?"

This was too much for Emma to consider, the idea of Merlin as a boy. She changed the subject. "Is that a real unicorn?" she asked.

"He's not pretend, if that's what you're asking," said Merlin. "And he's not a real lion or a real hoot owl, in which case, he must be a real unicorn. Right, Jeffrey?"

Jeffrey the unicorn nodded a ponyish version of yes and went back to his lunch.

"And what about her?" asked Roy, gesturing at the queen, who was laughing as she chased down a particularly large purple and gold specimen. "Last time, she was a lot less friendly."

"Ah, sorry about that. I was asleep and didn't know what was happening. I heard about it when she woke me up. A misunderstanding. Yes, she can be rather—ah—difficult. She gets lonely, and that lends itself to insecurity and meanness. When she isn't feeling her nerves, she's—" He looked over.

"Yes?" asked Emma.

"Not that bad," said Merlin.

Susan shifted from foot to foot, waiting for the pleasantries to be over. Finally she got impatient. "Merlin," she said, "we came because I have a question. Can I ask you my question?"

"You just did," said Merlin.

"Uh, no. I mean another one," said Susan. "About the magic." She continued quickly so that the wizard wouldn't have a chance to say no. "I was just wondering why things aren't wrapping up for us."

"Wrapping up?" asked Merlin.

"Yes. In books, the magic wraps itself up, fixes things, especially for kids."

"Ah, I see what you're driving at." The wizard smiled.

Susan went on. "That hasn't happened for us. We used the magic, and found this dog." Susan pointed to Bernice, still sitting, soggy, in the wagon. "But now we have nowhere to put her. We can't keep her, and the grown-up who was watching her gave her back to us, so what I want to know is why we still have this problem. Why isn't the magic taking care of her, wrapping up the loose ends for us?"

"Ah," said Merlin, crouching down to help Bernice from the wagon. He patted her head and said, "This is a very good question. I have two answers for you."

"Two?" asked Susan.

"The first is that the magic doesn't do anything for you. Fate can only take you so far; the rest is up to you."

"What do you mean?" asked Henry.

"I mean that in life, magic or not, there are a certain number of things you're sure to encounter," explained the wizard.

"Like the visions we saw?" asked Roy.

"Precisely like that," said Merlin. "But as I explained before, what you do with them and where they'll take you is not predetermined. You must think of life as a hallway filled with different doors. You are sure to see all the doors, but what happens to you at each turn depends on which door you open. Each door you open leads to a new hallway, and in each hallway, you'll find more doors. Again and again . . . to infinity. Infinite doors and infinite futures. Magic can transport you to a door, and a vision can give you a taste of what you'll find behind it, but you still have to make choices. Nothing is ever completely fixed."

"But what does all that have to do with Bernice?" asked Emma, her arm around the dog's neck.

"Well, you opened a door and found Bernice, right? You had a choice, and you chose to bring her home with you." He looked at Roy. "You accepted that responsibility when you rescued her, didn't you? You could have just as easily left her behind—"

"Hey! How do you know that?" asked Roy.

"I know most things," said Merlin.

"So what now?" asked Henry.

"Now you have to open another door. You have to seek the correct solution. Ask for help."

"But we did," said Susan. "We did ask for help. We asked Lily."

"Sometimes you have to try more than one door before you find what you seek," said Merlin.

"But how do we find the right door?" asked Roy, puzzled. "How do we figure it out?" He looked down at Bernice and wrinkled his forehead.

"Sometimes you can't figure things out so clearly," said Merlin. "Sometimes you just have to try a few doors, make a mistake or two."

Roy didn't like that idea.

Susan started to say something, but she shut her mouth. Then she opened it again. Then she closed it.

Merlin looked down at her and finished wiping his face clean. "Go on, Susan," he said softly. "Go ahead and try the door."

"Wait!" said Susan. "You said there were two things. What's the second?"

"Ah, the second," said Merlin. "The second is that in any story—bear in mind that we are all living out stories—the solution tends to come right at the end, where it belongs. Things don't wrap up midway through a tale. That's just bad narrative. No book can resolve in its own middle."

Susan chewed on this for a minute. Then she said

slowly, "So, if we opened the right door, asked the right person to take Bernice, and that person said yes and things were fixed, then the story of Bernice might be over?"

"That particular story, yes," said Merlin. "But then another story would begin. There are often sequels in life."

Susan considered this. "And certain, ah—other stories connected to Bernice, they might be over too?"

"You never can tell," said Merlin gently. "Everything is connected."

"Hmmmm." Susan eyed Merlin suspiciously.

Merlin eyed her back, but there was a tiny smile at the corner of his mouth. "Care to try me?" he asked.

"I'm thinking," said Susan.

"Well, that's good news," said Merlin. "You've learned something, anyway."

Bored with the length of the conversation, the others drifted off to see the unicorn.

"Okay," said Susan, taking a deep breath. "Here goes nothing."

Merlin rubbed his hands together and waited.

"I wonder if," Susan said, "maybe you'd like to take care of—"

"Yes?" Merlin asked. "Take care of—"

"Bernice!" blurted out Susan. "Would you like Bernice?"

Merlin grinned, as though he'd just won a game of checkers. "I have," he said, "always been partial to large dogs."

Susan let out a sigh, but whether it was a sigh of relief or disappointment, she wasn't sure. She handed Merlin the leash.

"We won't need that here," said Merlin. He undid the dog's collar, and Bernice gratefully gave the wizard's newly shaven cheek a big lick. Then she bounded off, truly free for the first time in her entire life, to steal the unicorn's food. Her limp was completely gone.

Across the yard, the others saw what was happening and ran back to where Susan and Merlin stood together.

"Merlin's going to keep her," said Susan. "Is that okay, Emma?"

"Oh, Bernice," said Emma sadly, watching the dog romp. "I'll miss you so much."

"We all will." Roy nodded.

"She's a good old dog," said Henry.

"Merlin," asked Susan, speaking more quietly than before. "Can I ask you something else?"

The wizard gazed kindly down at her, and this time didn't tease and say "You just did." His voice was gentle when he asked, "What is it, Susan?"

"How did you learn to be . . . you?"

"What else could I ever be?" said Merlin.

"No, I mean, you live in a weird shack all by yourself, and you're kind of, um, filthy?"

"Yes, that's true," said the wizard.

"Plus you're alone a lot, and there's nobody else like you in the world to keep you company, but you seem so happy."

"I can only be what I am," said Merlin. "And I'm happy, I suppose, because I don't try to be anything else. I know myself. Do you see?"

"I guess so," said Susan.

"You can't expect to be other than you are," said the wizard. "It's a lot of work to pretend. Just like your magic wall has to remain a wall, and can only turn into other walls, people have to remain who they are. They can change the way they look, their outsides, maybe, but the essence of who they are never changes. Walls, people, even beasts. Why, look at Jeffrey! He can only be Jeffrey. You think he had it easy with the other foals in the pasture, living with an elephant tusk protruding from his head? Of course he didn't, but he decided that instead of being a weird-looking horse, he'd be a unicorn. He invented himself."

"What do you mean, invented?" asked Henry. "You mean he was the very first unicorn?"

"I mean that he was, and remains, the *only* unicorn," said Merlin. "The only one that ever was. I found him about a thousand years ago, or last month, depending on how you're counting time. He's a freak of nature, Jeffrey is, but a nice one. Every story you've ever heard about a unicorn was based on Jeffrey! He's where the legend came from. An accident of a horse and a full moon, or that's my best guess. Every unicorn tale since has sprung from his story, just as every myth springs from something real."

"Oh my," said Emma. This was a lot to think about.

"And now," said Merlin, whistling the dog to his side, "that Bernice is here, I think it's time for us to go."

"Where are you going?" asked Susan.

"Not me, my dear, we," said Merlin, waving his hands in the air. "As you've clearly surmised, things are wrapping up."

And then, though none of them had been touching the wall, suddenly they were back in their field, at home, in Iowa. Merlin and Bernice were there too, standing in the shadow of the wall. The rain was gone, but a few gray clouds remained.

"It's time," said Merlin, "to say goodbye to your wall.

You've reached the last chapter of this particular story."

"Aw, no," said Henry. "No way. Finders, keepers. It's ours."

Merlin shook his head.

"Will anything magic ever happen again?" asked Emma.

"Of course," said the wizard. "Magic happens every day."

"No, she means to us," said Roy.

Merlin looked down at Roy thoughtfully, his gaze sincere and wise. The wizard inclined his head just the slightest bit, but instead of raising his eyes, he cocked his head to one side and closed his eyes for a moment, thinking deeply (or maybe just resting his lids).

The kids held their breath until Merlin opened his eyes and answered.

"I think," he said, "you will discover that once you have found magic, or rather, once magic has found you, it is not unlikely that you will stumble upon magic again. Because now you have learned to see the magic."

"You mean there's more magic?" asked Roy. "Other kinds of magic around?"

"It is everywhere, magic," said Merlin. "Always, and in the commonest places. Only most people don't know what they're looking for."

For no reason that any of them could see, Bernice barked sharply.

"Will we always know how to see it?" asked Susan, more quietly than usual. "Even when we get . . . older?"

Merlin sighed. "Some outgrow magic," he said sadly, "it's true, but some people never lose it. They keep it with them always, and it becomes a part of who they are. You can usually tell a person who has kept it with them. They're a little—different." As he said this, a few wildflower petals fell from his cloak and landed on the ground. They were purple, almost exactly the color of Lily's front porch.

"Enough chitchat! No reason to delay the inevitable," said Merlin. "THE END!" As he spoke these two final words, he patted the wall, struck it firmly with the flat of his hand.

And then the wall, the huge wall, began to tumble. The kids gasped at the movement of the stones and their strange descent. They drifted, slowly and lightly, as though the wall were made of feathers. As the stones fell, they seemed to flatten and become two-dimensional. They fluttered like sheets of paper to the ground. When they hit the grass, they disappeared like snowflakes. They were there one second and gone the next.

When it was over, Merlin turned his back on them

and looked off into the field. "Keep the key," he said.

Henry, startled, reached into his pocket and pulled out the key. He held it flat on his palm and stared at it. They all did, and while they were looking down, Merlin began to walk away, whistling. Bernice bounded after him, as happy as a dog can be.

"Bernice!" cried Emma. She blew a kiss.

"Will we see you again?" called out Roy. "Ever?"

"Who knows?" the wizard called back over his shoulder. "Besides me, I mean." He chuckled as he made his way through the field.

They all watched the wizard and the dog grow smaller and smaller. At last Henry said, "I wonder why he's walking. Why doesn't he fly or something?"

Roy shrugged. "Maybe he just likes to walk."

Then, in the distance, Bernice gave a delighted woof, and it was as though a spell was suddenly broken. Henry, Emma, Susan, and Roy looked around and found that the day was, well, there. The sun was peering from behind a cloud, and a faint breeze tickled them with rain. Overhead, a red-winged blackbird darted joyfully, with rapid bursts of fluttering wings. The field was green and lush and it was summertime in Iowa.

"Ha!" shouted Henry. "Last one home makes lunch!"

And they all began to run.

GREAT THANKS——

To the memory of the incomparable Edward Eager.

To the city of Iowa City, the real Quiet Falls.

To my Iowa family, the Pomas. I'm grateful and lucky to have married into such a clan.

To the friends of my Iowa years, who haunted the writing of this book—especially Thisbe Nissen, Sarah Townsend, Sonya Naumann, Annie Crawford, Atom Robinson, Kelly Pardekooper, Patrick Brickell, Dave Olson, Jeff Skinner, Jerry Sorokin, Steve Fugate, Mindy Ash, Margaret Schwartz, Sharone Levy, and Pieta and Constie Brown.

To my Atlanta friends, who made it possible to deliver a manuscript and a baby in the same year—Abbie Gulson, Elizabeth Lenhard, Joanna Davidson, Shenandoah Evans, Noelle York-Simmons, Amy Dingler, Emily Capps, Laurie Watel, Amanda French, and Aimee Goodman. And to Janet McKee, Jordan Ainsley, Emily Martin, Cindy Cahalen, and TeShaye Elder—who took good care of my boys so I could write.

To James Staub, Maria Weidener, Stacy Oborn, and Jacqui Carper, who know me.

To Tina Wexler, my agent, who tells the truth and has the very best laugh.

To my inspired editor, Mallory Loehr, who is not at all mimsy, and puts me at ease.

To Ellice Lee for making the words into an actual object. To LeUyen Pham for her genius and her humor. To Alison Kolani for understanding italics. And to Kate Klimo, Jim Thomas, Whitney Stahlberg, Chelsea Eberly, Elizabeth Daniel, and all the other good folks at Random House, who have managed to disprove every negative stereotype I had about the business of publishing.

To the insane and fabulous women of the poet_moms Listserv, my mirrors. To Jennifer Laughran, who holds her thumbs for me, and Sarah Prineas, who is tricky. To Marc Fitten, who knows that pretend lunch meetings are the best kind. To Summer Laurie and Nicole Geiger, who took a chance.

To my family—Kate Hamill and Steve Gettinger, Steve Snyder and Cheryl Hindes, Henry, Emma, and Roy Snyder, Judy and Gene Goldstein. With great love.

To Paul Kaplan and Nancy Quade, who tuck me in and make no fuss and let me say anything.

To the memory of Ann Dietz. Grandmother, children's librarian, and exotic bird.

And of course and always—to Chris, Mose, and Lewis Poma. My boys.

About the
Author and Illustrator

LAUREL SNYDER spent seven magical years in a town just like Quiet Falls, but then she fell under a spell and was whisked away. She is currently searching hard for a wishing wall to transport her back to the cornfields. While she waits, she contents herself with writing books like *Up and Down the Scratchy Mountains* and *Inside the Slidy Diner*, imagining that her house is clean, and chasing after one husband, two little boys, and a very surly cat named Hassle. *Any Which Wall* is her second novel.

LeUYEN PHAM travels far and wide in search of adventure when she leaves the four walls of her studio. When inside those walls, she relies on her imagination and paintbrush to take her to amazing places. Her magic has made many award-winning books, including the Alvin Ho series, *Freckleface Strawberry* by Julianne Moore, *God's Dream* by Archbishop Desmond Tutu, and her very own *Big Sister, Little Sister*. She lives in magical San Francisco with her wizard husband, Alex, and their little elf, Leo.